Rubber-Band Ball

The Mason Braithwaite Paranormal
Mystery Series, book 5

In this series:

Signs Point to Yes

The Desert Rats

Reach for the Sky

Billy Blood

Rubber-Band Ball

The Invisible Arrow

Penstock Canyon

The Man from Grapalia

The Mythical Blond

Stealth Glasses

The Melted Pineapple

Night on the Water

The Landers Mystique

Rubber-Band Ball

Rubber-Band Ball

Christopher Church

DAGMAR
MIURA
LOS ANGELES

Published by Dagmar Miura
Los Angeles
www.dagmarmiura.com

Rubber-Band Ball

First published 2017

ISBN: 978-1-942267-19-5

ONE

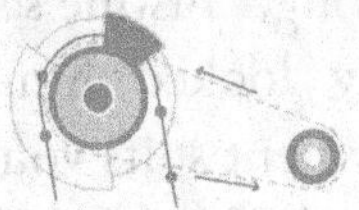

Having a boyfriend who was in recovery, Mason didn't hang out in bars very often. Now that he thought about it, he didn't know if he'd ever hung out in a sports bar before. Justine had summoned him to this one in a busy part of Pasadena, a schlep from his own neighborhood on the train. She didn't live anywhere near here either, so presumably her uncle, the potential client, did.

It felt good to get out of his familiar routine, and Mason nursed a pint of pale ale while he waited. He twisted around on his barstool, amused by the Saturday crowd of affluent suburbanites—contented in their privilege, laughing with their friends, roaring at the esoteric developments of the ball game on the video screens. There weren't any places like this in his more urban neighborhood. He scanned the entryway for Justine, then stretched and turned back to his beer.

A minute or two later he caught sight of her walking in, followed by an older guy who was wearing a sport coat despite the warm day. She had already seen him, a broad smile on her face. Mason wasn't hard to spot—even sitting on a barstool he was a head taller than most people, and then there was his shock of red hair. He slid off the barstool and squared his shoulders.

"It's been too long," Justine said as she embraced him, then quickly looked him over. "You look good—self-employment suits you."

"You got that right," he said.

She smiled. "Uncle Steve, this is Mason," she said, putting a hand on Mason's shoulder.

"You don't have to call me 'uncle,'" he said, smiling and meeting Mason's eye. "Steve works fine."

"A pleasure," Mason said. "Let's sit."

Mason grabbed his beer and followed them through the crowd toward the tables in back. He remembered that Justine had called Steve "eccentric but harmless," but so far he seemed personable enough.

Justine found a little round table and they all got comfortable. The waitress greeted Steve by name. He and Justine both ordered draft beer.

"Justine tells me you used to work together at the gossip website," Steve said.

"We did," Mason said, "although that seems like a hundred years ago."

"I was there on Mason's last day," she said, grinning at the memory. "I cleaned out your desk after you stormed out of there."

Steve laughed. "That sounds dramatic."

"It kind of was," Mason admitted. "I was ready to leave."

"You look different now," Justine said. "Calmer, maybe."

"That's not surprising. I get to sleep in." But Mason knew a lot more than that had changed since that day. Working for himself, doing work he believed in, he'd discovered a drive he never knew he had.

The waitress set their drinks on the table, and the three of them clinked glasses. Steve watched Mason as they drank, quietly assessing him.

"Justine tells me you find yourself in need of a psychic investigator," Mason said, setting his glass down.

"That's right," Steve said, leaning forward. "Do you know anything about ley lines?"

"I've heard of them, I think—it's about earth energy, right?"

"Exactly."

Justine frowned. "I thought you wanted help with real estate. What on earth are ley lines?"

"Real estate is part of it," Steve said. "Ley lines are energy pathways that crisscross the earth." He turned back to Mason, holding his gaze. "I need help locating them."

"Hasn't someone mapped them out already?" Mason asked. "If I've heard of them, they must have."

"You can't really map them because they move around. You know how tectonic plates move a little every year? They're like that, but a little faster."

"OK," Mason said. It was an odd request, but it might be something he could do. "How many are there?"

Steve's eyes grew wide. "Lots. There are major ones and minor ones, stronger and weaker. They shift over time, and wax and wane in power, but they're always perfectly straight lines."

"Why do you need to find them?" Justine asked, looking dubious.

"We'll get to that," Steve said. "A lot of people believe that there are several first-order ley lines running under LA—at least two, maybe three. It's part of why this big city is here, and why there's so much activity going on."

"What people?" Justine asked, shifting uncomfortably in her chair.

"People who are sensitive to them," he said intently. "People like Mason."

Mason could see understanding in Steve's eyes, the shared knowledge that there was more to the world than what was outwardly visible. "I'm willing to look into it," he said.

"Good," Steve said, and nodded emphatically.

Justine took a long drink of her lager.

"Where two lines cross, it's called a node," Steve

said. "Those are pretty common. But where three lines cross, it's called a supernode—and there might be one near here." He looked intently at Mason. "I want you to find it."

"What are you going to do with a supernode?" Justine asked.

"First things first," Steve said, looking at her. "Let's find out if it even exists."

Justine looked to Mason expectantly.

"I'm in," Mason said. "I can't promise results, but I'll do my best."

"Great," Steve said. "I suppose I should ask what it's going to cost me."

"For research, I usually charge five hundred a day," Mason said.

Justine's eyebrows shot up, but Steve just nodded.

"Before I can give you an idea how long it might take, I need to figure out how to approach the problem," Mason said. "Can I do some groundwork and let you know?"

"Absolutely," Steve said, and clinked his glass against Mason's. "Here's to psychic power."

"Cheers," Mason said.

Justine quickly changed the subject, updating Mason on his former coworkers, and they chatted about her social life and Mason's boyfriend, Ned. When Steve excused himself to go to the men's room, she leaned closer to Mason and said, "I had no idea his thing was so far-out. He was talking about buying land, so I thought maybe he wanted you to check out the juju on the house or something."

Mason grinned. "I can handle far-out. It's my specialty."

"So I don't need to be embarrassed by my crazy uncle?"

"Of course not. He doesn't seem crazy at all. I like him—he's upbeat, like you are."

"There's only one Uncle Steve," she said.

"Lucky for you," Steve said as he sat down again, putting a hand on her shoulder. He turned to Mason. "Can I get your phone number? I'll text you back with mine."

Mason recited the number, and a moment later he felt his phone buzz in his pants pocket. He pulled it out to check; he'd texted his name, "Steve Glaser."

"Got it," Mason told him.

When they rose to leave, Justine gave Mason a hug, and he followed them out to the street, waving good-bye and then stopping at a coffee joint to slam a double espresso. The beer had made him sleepy.

The metro was a few blocks away. He boarded a train and settled into a seat by the window to watch the mountains and the well-manicured neighborhoods roll by on the way back to the gritty concrete heart of the city. Ley lines were intriguing, but he wasn't sure how to approach the job. Not knowing had never stopped him before, though.

Steve was affable, and his ask seemed straightforward, but he'd never answered Justine's question about why he wanted to find this supernode. He'd even seemed cagey about it. He could ask for more details before leading Steve to it, Mason decided, to make sure Steve was on the up-and-up—assuming he found it at all.

Perhaps he could get some insight into Steve psychically. Mason closed his eyes and tuned out the sounds of the train, clearing his mind, sweeping away the random thoughts that came up. He focused on Steve, remembering his face and his posture. "What's this guy all about?" he thought, and waited for insight, something that came from elsewhere, beyond the chatter of his mind.

It took a while, but eventually an image formed—a dark disk. Suddenly it became lit at one edge by a white crescent, expanding slowly. It was the moon, Mason realized, rapidly running through its phases. It reached full brightness and then started to wane again. Mason concentrated on the image, but once he was sure there wasn't anything to it beyond the moon and its phases, he let it go. It didn't seem to relate to Steve or anything else.

He changed trains downtown and soon climbed the stairs up out of the station near home, finding his bicycle still in the rack where he'd locked it up. After cycling up into his hilly LA neighborhood in the summer heat, he was drenched with sweat when he dismounted and opened the garage. Both Ned's cars were inside, so he had to be in. Ned worked from home but on Saturday he was often out running errands.

When he pushed open the front door, Ned was sitting on a stool at the counter that separated the kitchen from the living room.

"Hey, sweets," Ned said, looking up from the binder of recipes in front of him.

Mason loved coming home to this guy. He was shorter and slighter than Mason, and had dark hair and Latin features. And he always looked sharp—Ned looked more polished when he rolled out of bed than Mason could after an hour of highly focused grooming.

"Hey," Mason said, and stepped over to kiss him hello.

"How was your meeting?" Ned asked, twisting around to face him.

"Good, I think," Mason said. "Dude seems reasonable."

"Not that hiring a psychic is inherently reasonable," Ned said.

Mason wanted to brush off the skepticism, but it was hard. Even after Mason had shown that he could successfully make a living this way, Ned wasn't convinced that Mason had any skills beyond old-fashioned library research and mundane deductive reasoning. Ned was a committed nontheist, and he refused to consider any idea that couldn't be backed up by scientific evidence.

"Not that you're the arbiter of what reasonable is," Mason said.

Ned laughed. "Fair enough. What does he want

you to do? Did you take the job?"

Mason sat at the counter with him and explained Steve's request.

"I've never even heard of ley lines," Ned said. "But I guess if they're invisible, you can just point them out and present an invoice. How can the guy argue whether they're there or not?"

"They're invisible, but they are real," Mason said, pushing aside his exasperation and keeping his tone even. "The issue is whether or not I can find them."

"As long as you get paid."

"I'm sure I will—he didn't balk when I laid out my rates. And the best part is, it doesn't seem like the kind of job where someone's going to pull a knife on me."

"Given your track record, I wouldn't rule it out," Ned said dubiously.

Mason gestured to the recipe binder to change the subject. "Are you looking for something to make for dinner?"

"I'm thinking this soup of my auntie's, remember? With the pearl barley thrown in at the end?"

"Oh, that is a good soup," Mason said. Mason and Ned were both vegan, which was one of the reasons they'd gotten together. In the few years they'd lived together, Ned had become an accomplished vegan cook.

"Can you ask Peggy if she'll be home for dinner?" Ned said.

They often ate dinner with their roommate,

Peggy, except when she had to be out for a gig. She had a day job, but her true passion was the unique folk music she performed in coffeehouses and bars around town. Mason texted her,

> Aunt Alma's pearl barley soup for dinner. Are you dining here?

A minute later her reply came back:

> Nope. Busy. Enjoy.

He relayed this to Ned, then left him to his cooking and went down the hall to the office they shared. The room was dark, and since it was still nice outside, he grabbed his computer and went out to the balcony, looking out over the neighborhood, drenched in the late-day sun.

Lots had been written about ley lines, he found after some online searching, but none of it was very substantive. The idea seemed to have originated in Britain, where ley lines were said to run between significant cathedrals, castles, and monuments. But no one was sure whether the lines had been there first and had attracted the construction, or whether human activity had generated them. One researcher was convinced that most of coastal California was a broad energetic zone where creativity was accelerated by earth energy. That probably had more to do with the people living here than what lurked underground, Mason thought, but he read through it anyway, along with an array of other content that ranged from the pseudoscientific to the blindly religious. He found references to a couple of books that might have more information, but he'd have to go to the library for those.

An hour later Ned pushed open the French doors. "Soup's on," he said.

They ate at the dining room table, and the soup was delicious, thick and chunky with chewy barley. Ned served it with a loaf of crusty Italian bread that he'd made, and Mason ate with gusto.

"Peggy has no idea what she's missing," he said.

After dinner he cleaned up and left Ned sprawled on the sofa with a novel, then sat at his desk and pulled out a yellow notepad to record what he'd learned. "Steve Glaser," he wrote across the top of the page, and "Ley Lines and Nodes." He thought for a moment, and then crossed out "Nodes" and wrote "Supernodes."

He jotted down notes about what he'd found, and then scanned it again; it wasn't much. He should probably ask someone with practical knowledge, perhaps a peer in his field. The obvious choice was Hanh, a psychic who had helped Mason once when he'd been stuck; he'd returned the favor later on by joining a séance that she'd organized. More than just a psychic practitioner, she also seemed to oversee other psychics, specifically the ones who had the ability to slip through time. Bizarrely, she also ran the nail salon where Ned got his manicures. She was never very forthcoming with information, though—whenever he'd queried her about the mechanics of their psychic experiences, she'd replied in the vein of "figure it out your damn self."

It had to be someone more communicative. At Hanh's séance he'd met a woman named Anna, and she had seemed fairly pragmatic and happy to chat. She'd called herself a storefront psychic, and Mason remembered her mentioning that her shop was on Olympic Boulevard. He pulled open his laptop and soon found it—not far away, and in a retail space. She'd probably be working late on a Saturday. He decided to go, even though there wasn't a lot of daylight left. He was afraid to ride in the dark, but he could get most of the way there on the metro.

He stuffed his notepad into his backpack and slung it over his shoulders, then told Ned where he was headed. Mounting his bike, he soared down the hill to the boulevard, elated by the cool evening air and the feeling of purpose the new job gave him. He carried his bike down with him to the train, and soon he was in the neighborhood, riding on quiet side streets and then the sidewalk when he neared her business, searching for the building numbers. Cars whizzed by on the boulevard, but the sidewalk was deserted; the strip she was on was seedy, ungentrified, with heavy steel shutters covering storefronts, paint peeling on wooden trim. Her front window announced PALM READING and TAROT in neon orange glare that he spotted a block away, and just in case that wasn't clear, emblazoned on the awning above in large lettering was PSYCHIC. He had to smile. No one would mistake Anna as shy about her vocation.

When he rolled up, sure enough, the sign read OPEN. He locked his bicycle to a parking sign a few doors down. A little bell tinkled as he opened the door and walked into the tiny room. There were two chairs, a little statue of a deity on a low table—Guanyin, he knew, but he couldn't remember what she represented; compassion, maybe, or something similarly weighty—and on the wall a poster of a fuzzy flying saucer photo with the caption KEEP YOUR EYES ON THE SKIES. The room was draped in black velour, lit only by the ambient glow of the sign hanging in the window. He stood for a moment, listening to the electric buzz of the neon and the muffled traffic outside, and considered shouting "Hello?" through the purple fabric hanging in the doorway opposite the window, but before he could, a young woman stepped through the curtains and greeted him with a smile. She couldn't have been more than eighteen, and wore jeans and a T-shirt. Deftly pulling her hair back, she secured it with an elastic, as if preparing for physical labor.

"Welcome," she said, and gestured to one of the chairs. "Have a seat."

"I'm actually here to see Anna," Mason said.

"I can get her," she said, "but first, can you show me your palm?"

"OK," Mason said, and held out his hand, palm

up. She took it in both hands and peered at it carefully, her brow deeply knitted.

"There are some serious things going on in your life," she said finally, looking up at him with an expression of concern. "I really think you should sit down."

"I don't need a reading," Mason said, smiling at her sincerity.

"You can't afford not to," she said. "Besides, the initial consultation is only ten bucks."

Mason laughed and pulled off his backpack, setting it between his feet as he sat in one of the chairs. It was illuminating to see how other psychics worked, and despite the lurid lighting and dusty drapery, he was pulled in by her dramatic pitch.

She sat across from him and took his hand once again, brushing it gently with her little finger, as if it were covered in numinous cobwebs. She looked up suddenly and locked eyes with him.

"Someone in your office is trying to undermine you," she said sharply, not breaking her gaze, her hands still firmly gripping his.

"I don't work in an office," Mason said slowly, shaking his head.

"Your coworkers," she insisted. "Someone is trying to sabotage you."

"I work for myself," he said. "I don't really have any coworkers."

She looked back to his palm, peering into it for a few moments, then looked intensely at him again and said, "Someone is trying to interfere in your love life."

"Hmm … I've been with the same guy for a few years now, and we're pretty stable. I can't imagine anyone would be trying to mess with that."

She looked at his palm again, pulling it closer to her face, massaging it as she scanned it. "Someone is trying to harm your family," she said, locking eyes with him again.

"You know, I don't really have any enemies," Mason said, shrugging.

"You need a deeper reading," she said, finally releasing his hand. "Do you have a hundred dollars today to make your life safer?"

Before he could respond, Anna stepped through the purple curtains. "Mason," she said. "What are you doing here?" With her accent, which seemed vaguely Eastern European, she pronounced his name "*may*-seen." When he'd met her before, she'd been dressed like an ordinary person, but tonight she was dressed for work: a dark floral scarf tied over her hair and a burgundy caftan over her bulky frame, a dramatic crystal necklace sparkling in the dim light.

He and the young woman both stood up. "I'm here to see you, but I got a palm reading too," he said.

Anna cackled. "Come on in," she said, and ducked back through the purple curtains.

He pulled his cash out of his hip pocket and peeled off a ten-dollar bill, handing it to the young woman with a grin before grabbing his backpack and following Anna. In the back was another consultation room, this one larger but also heavily draped in black, a round table in the middle surrounded by folding chairs. Anna pushed through another curtained doorway farther back, this time into an undecorated space with a desk and a mini fridge.

"Coffee?" she asked, gesturing to a battered and stained coffeemaker on the counter beside the sink.

"It's a bit late for me, but thanks," Mason said.

"Sit," she said, waving to the chairs beside the table. She poured herself half a mug from the grimy machine and sank into the other chair.

"Who is that young woman?" he asked.

"My niece," Anna said, waving a hand dismissively. "She's learning the trade. We all have rent to pay."

"I get it," Mason said, and smiled.

"So, is Hanh planning another séance?" she asked.

"No—I dropped by because I wanted to see if you know anything about ley lines."

"Not a lot. I know they're around. For us, though, they're basically useless."

"What do you mean?"

"Well, they're energy lines, but we can't draw energy from them. You won't get better psychic vibes even if you're standing right on top of one. They have no effect on ESP."

"I see. Do you know how to detect them?"

"I've never tried." She sized him up for a moment, knitting her brow. "I'm sure you have the ability. You're one of us, and you're getting money."

Mason chuckled, and sat up straighter. "That's true."

"The ley lines are from England, right?"

"They are, but I want to find some around here."

"Have you tried the tarot cards? As a general tool, I mean."

"I've played around with them, but the information I got was too general. Lucid dreaming works better for me, and reading objects."

"So you're going to do a psychometry reading on the whole entire earth to find the ley lines?" she said, raising her eyebrows. "I don't think so. Ask the cards. They're very powerful."

"I guess I could do a tarot reading. I have a deck at home."

"Let me do a reading for you now," she said, and before he could reply she rose and ducked back into the consultation room. She returned a moment later with a well-worn deck of cards in hand, then pushed the magazines and unopened mail on the table into a pile and set the cards in the cleared space.

"Past, future, or both?" she asked, sitting down again.

"Not the past—I've already been there. What I need is insight into the case I'm working."

"All right," she said. "Shuffle the deck, and think about your question."

He picked up the cards and saw that they were the standard Rider-Waite deck, used by generations of seers before Anna. He shuffled them briefly and set them down. Anna fanned out the cards with a flourish, spreading them across the table.

"Pick four," she said, "and turn them over."

The first was the Page of Wands, and then came the Queen of Cups, the Moon, and the Ten of Coins. Mason laid them out in a row above the others.

Anna assessed the spread. "You've got some work ahead of you."

"What do you see?" he asked.

"You're going to cross paths with a couple of women, and become entangled with them. There is deceit." She thought for a moment, staring at the cards, furrowing her brow. "Maybe not deceit. Secrets, and deception. You'll think you understand, but you won't. You won't be told the whole truth."

He smiled. "That happens a lot in my line of work. Does the Page represent me?"

She shook her head. "It's a woman. She has big plans, and you'll help her achieve them. And this one," she tapped the Queen of Cups, "is an old woman. She might help you, if you can approach her in the right way."

It sounded nebulous to Mason, and imprecise, the way the tarot always did.

"I wonder what the right way will be?" he said lightly, not really expecting an answer.

Anna met his eye. "Her family. Talk about her relatives, and she'll begin to trust you."

He couldn't see how that tied in to the question of ley lines, but he knew he couldn't dismiss it. He'd seen Anna at work before, and her insight was as valid as his own.

"This one, though," she said, tapping the Page of Wands, "is sincere. You'll be able to trust her from the beginning."

"What about the Moon? It's the only major card that came up."

"It speaks to the idea of deception, things long buried, and the two people you'll get involved with. These are powerful women, and you can benefit from working with them. But it won't be easy."

"Thanks," he said, sitting back in his chair as she flipped the cards over again and gathered up the deck.

"The power of the cards goes far beyond this room," she said, leaning toward him, her eyes gleaming. "You have to look at your environment, the people around you, and the questions you have, and find the characteristics of the cards in your surroundings. Reflecting on that will blow your mind."

He smiled at the expressive phrase. "It's an interesting idea. I'll try it out."

"Do," she said firmly, and briefly squeezed his knee, looking him in the eye. "Remember—you're surrounded by the cards all the time."

"Got it," Mason said, meeting her gaze. She was serious about this.

In the distance he heard the tinkle of the bell over the front door, and a moment later Anna's niece stepped through the curtain.

"Your 8:30 is here," she said.

"Work," Anna said, rising from her chair and smiling apologetically.

"The rent," he said, standing up as well.

"Can you show yourself out the back? My clients don't like to run into each other. Confidentiality issues. You understand."

"Of course," he said, and thanked her again.

"It was nice to meet you," the young woman said, smiling sweetly now, no hint of her deep concern for the peril she had perceived in his palm.

"Same here," he said, and nodded good-bye.

He found the heavy fire door at the back of the shop and pushed it open, then walked around the building and found his bicycle, switched on its lights, and cycled back to the metro.

Both of them had been intense, and the young woman's hard sell had clearly been just that, not a true psychic reading. It wasn't the best face of his profession, using fear to sell. More than anything, it built skepticism. But as Anna had said, they had to make a living. She seemed like a nice kid, and hopefully wouldn't abuse her clients' credulity too much. And Anna—she was so enthusiastic that her reading would help him get psychic insight. It sounded tenuous, but he intended to look into it anyway.

"There's a new *Pica Confessions,*" Ned said when Mason walked into the house. It was one of the few television programs they watched. "It's about this guy who eats the colored gravel that goes in the bottom of a fish tank. He buys it by the pound."

"That does sound amazing," Mason said, slipping off his backpack, "but I want to do some work. I'll leave you to it."

He sat at his desk and got comfortable, then did a Web search for Steve Glaser. A lot of results popped up, but when he added "Los Angeles" as a search term he was able to find Uncle Steve. A business profile listed him as a marine metallurgist, which looked to be some kind of mechanical engineer. He worked for a Korean shipping business at the port, which seemed odd until he read about the company. It employed hundreds of people locally and did a lot of trade.

It was always surprising to see how people's lives, and the world in general, were differentiated into such specific tasks and enterprises, like a job working with the metal composition of a cargo ship's fittings, or a globe-spanning company he'd never heard of. There was so much going on in this town.

He pulled his notepad out of his backpack and added a few lines about Steve. It was reassuring to find out more about the guy. The fact that he had an ordinary job didn't mean he wasn't interested in ley lines for some odious purpose, but having a fuller picture of who he was helped put Mason's mind at ease.

He leaned back and rubbed his eyes; it was getting late. Folding his computer closed, he went down the hall to their bedroom. Peggy's room was open and empty as he walked by. She wasn't out performing, because her guitar was propped against the wall, but maybe tomorrow she'd reveal more than her terse text had.

He peeled off his clothes and crawled into bed. Ned was still awake and reading, but he put his tablet down and moved closer.

"How was the gravel-eating?" Mason asked.

"They made him confess to his boss, and the guy fired him on the spot. It seemed excessive. I think he just needed a little understanding."

"Why don't they ever send them to a shrink?" Mason asked.

"There's no entertainment value in that," he said.

One of the techniques Mason had found useful in obtaining extrasensory information was lucid dreaming, where he could come to awareness in the dream state. It didn't always work, and he often had trouble maneuvering inside dreams, but he'd obtained some fruitful leads.

Tonight he dreamed that he was in bed with moonlight streaming in the window. At first he wasn't sure if he was actually still awake, but no, it felt like a dream, the vivid blue-white rays of light almost vibrating as they illuminated the floor and bed. The bed started shaking, jostling his whole body, the whole room creaking and popping like it might fly apart. The window frame looked like it had turned to liquid, undulating with the quaking. He woke up breathing hard, fear flooding his body. This room, in the real world, was thankfully still, the window frame immobile in the wall, no moonlight visible.

He clicked the bedside lamp on and pulled a notepad out of the nightstand, squinting and scribbling notes about the experience. In his groggy state it didn't seem to mean anything, but he wanted to remember.

TWO

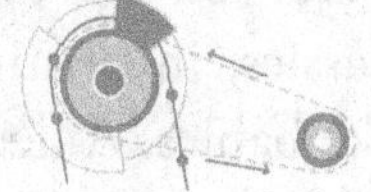

The best mornings were the ones with no alarm, when Mason could get up when his body wanted him to. He pulled on some clothes and went down to the kitchen, got the espresso machine going, and munched on some strawberries and an apple while he waited. He poured the whole pot of espresso into a mug and sat at the counter, appreciatively sipping the life-giving nectar.

He heard the garage door open and close; apparently Ned had been out. "Good morning," he called when Ned came in the front door. "Where were you?"

"I drove my mom to mass. Her car is in the shop."

He came over and kissed Mason hello.

"That was sweet of you. Did you go in with her, get a little salvation?"

"Are you kidding me? I went to a coffeehouse and picked her up after."

"I'm sure she appreciated it anyway," Mason said, taking a gulp of his espresso.

"It makes me feel like an enabler, helping her participate in that grandiose fairy tale, but yeah, she was grateful." He started unbuttoning his sleeves. "I'm going to change clothes and then detail the Barracuda. What are you up to today?" Both of Ned's cars were classics, in pristine condition, and he treated them like babies. A deep cleaning would take him all day.

"I'm off to the library, eventually. Is there a plan for dinner?"

"Peggy wanted to learn gazpacho, so we're going to do that together."

"I'll be here," Mason said, and drained his coffee before starting another pot.

Partway through the second cup, he felt awake enough to engage with the world. He took his phone out onto the balcony and settled into a chair. Anna hadn't been any help with ley lines, but he'd made another contact at Hanh's séance—a guy named Matt, who wasn't a psychic but worked in academia, and had lots of experience with psychic techniques. They'd developed some camaraderie when they'd collaborated on taking down a crooked soft-drink company. He dialed, and held the phone to his ear.

"What's up, motherfucker?" Matt answered cheerfully.

"Do you talk to your students like that?" Mason asked.

"Of course not. But I talk to you like that."

"I'm honored. Listen, I wanted to pick your brain about something."

"It's crazy that you called," Matt said. "I've got something for you too. You're a full-on vegan, right?"

"Now and forever."

"So meet me at that place on Sunset, and we'll shoot the shit. That one with all the cakes."

"I know the place you mean," Mason said, and they agreed to meet for lunch. The trip to the library would have to wait until later.

He finished his coffee and got dressed, then pulled on his backpack and went out to the garage. Ned was wearing old jeans and a tight white T-shirt, and had pulled his car out into the driveway to work in the daylight. He was just getting started, and the Barracuda was already gleaming and spotless. Rags, a bucket, and esoteric cleaning products lined the driveway. It was a timeless ritual, boys and their cars, and he wanted to stay and watch Ned doing something he loved. But not today.

"Have fun," Mason said, climbing onto his bicycle.

"Always," Ned said, and cheerfully kissed him good-bye.

Mason coasted down to the boulevard and made his way toward Sunset Junction. The café wasn't close to a station, so he had to ride all the way, but at least there was a bike lane on the busy boulevard. Matt was there when he walked in, at a little booth along the wall. He waved at Mason, and caught the waitress as she went by.

"A triple espresso for my friend here," he told her.

"Thanks," Mason said appreciatively, settling into the other seat, and added, "Bring me a slice of that berry layer cake too." When she'd gone, he asked Matt, "How did you know that was what I wanted?"

"It's what you always order." He grinned and added, "No psychic power necessary."

Mason didn't know the guy all that well, but it was nice that he remembered things like that. He liked Matt, he realized. "Is that what you wanted to talk to me about—psychic stuff?" Mason asked.

Matt nodded and sipped at his coffee. "Yeah, but you called me. You go first."

"OK. Do you know how to detect ley lines?"

"What the fuck are ley lines?" Matt asked.

Mason explained what he knew, and talked about meeting Steve.

"Interesting," Matt said. "What's dude going to do with the supernode when he finds it?"

"I have no idea. But he seems like a decent guy."

"That's what people always say about the psychopath next door after he gets arrested—'He seemed like a decent guy.' What if he wants to blow shit up?"

"I figured I'd assess that before passing on the information." Mason could feel his cheeks turning red.

"Definitely," Matt said, and then a look of concern came over his face. "Don't get steamed, man, it's just a thought."

"I'm not upset. It's the curse of the redhead, the pasty complexion—the slightest reaction is written all over my face." He shifted uncomfortably in his seat, and thanked the waitress when she set down his coffee and his cake.

Matt nodded. "Anyway, if it's an earth thing, I'd use astral projection. Have you ever tried that?"

"No," Mason said through a mouthful of cake.

"I've done it. It's easy to get to a specific physical location that way. No time shifting, though—it happens in real time."

"How does it work?"

"You basically learn to float around without your body. The hard part for me is that I get freaked out without my body and can't stay away for very long. But you can train yourself to get used to it."

"How do you do it?" Mason asked, putting his fork down and pulling his notepad out of his backpack.

"Well, you start somewhere quiet, like in bed, with your eyes closed, and then clear all the bullshit out of your mind. Then you tell your body you're going to detach. Like, 'I'm leaving, and I'll be back later.'"

Mason scribbled some notes.

Matt continued, "You'll start to float up out of your body. You'll know you're floating, and you'll be able to see where you are. It's easy to start floating, but it's fucking hard to stay up there. I get an irrational panicky urge to get back to my body. Once you're detached, you can think of a specific place, anywhere, and you're there. In your case, I'd just ask, 'Where are the ley lines?' Then you should be looking at them."

"It sounds doable," Mason said, still scribbling away. "Is it dangerous?"

"I saw you ride up on a goddamn bicycle, so you're obviously comfortable with a little danger, two-wheeling it in this town."

"But can you lose track of your body?" Mason asked, looking up at Matt.

"I doubt it. You only have to think about going back to your body, and there you are. You also don't ever really leave your body—it's just how your mind interprets probing a separate point in space."

"I guess that's reassuring," Mason said, absorbing it all and taking another mouthful of cake.

"In a way, I guess it is, but it's also kind of fucked. Your mind protects you from the true nature of reality. Our little monkey brains can't handle the complexity, so we perceive a simplified version.

Doesn't that seem a little sad?"

Mason thought about it for a minute, and then nodded. "Yeah, I guess it is," he said. But his concerns were more pragmatic. "So what was the thing you wanted to talk about?"

"Have you heard from Hanh lately?"

Mason shook his head. "What is her deal, exactly? She seems to be like a nanny for the psychics, or a cop."

"It's probably a little of both. But she saved my ass, and I'd do just about anything she asked of me. She has an errand for us."

"She saved mine too," Mason admitted. "I guess I owe her. But why didn't she call me herself?"

"Well … she didn't actually call. I kind of dreamed about it. So I'm not totally sure what she needs help with." Matt looked sheepish, and took a sip from his coffee cup.

"You don't have to be embarrassed about that," Mason said. "I'm working with the same toolkit, remember? If you got information that way, I'm sure it's valid."

"Thanks," Matt said, and nodded. "Not everyone is quite so open-minded. I'm sure you've faced plenty of skepticism too."

"Oh, yeah," Mason said. "My boyfriend, my shrink—even some of the people who hire me."

Matt laughed. "It's weird, right, to navigate the world with beliefs that are different from everyone else's?"

"Yes," Mason said emphatically. They spent a few minutes talking about their experiences while Mason finished his cake. Eventually Matt called the waitress to settle the bill.

"So if you find out what we're supposed to do for Hanh, call me," Mason said.

"And vice versa. All I know for sure is that it's coming up, and it involves both of us."

"Another thing," Mason said. "Are you single?"

Matt's eyes narrowed. "Why?"

"My roommate has been single for a while now, and you might like her."

"Is she nice?"

Mason laughed. "I am so glad that's the first thing you asked."

"What were you expecting?"

"A lot of guys would have asked whether she was hot."

"Is she hot?"

"That's completely subjective. Do you have a type?"

"I used to say my type was double-X chromosome, but then I dated this trans woman for a while, so I can't even say that anymore."

"Well, I don't know if you'll think she's hot, but she's definitely nice. She's also funny, and a wickedly talented musician, and not skeptical of my psychic abilities."

"That alone is attractive," Matt said. "What the hell—set me up. Just don't write me off as a prick when she decides she hates me."

Mason smiled. "You make it sound like that's the only possible outcome."

"There's an old saying," Matt said. "'Love stories usually end badly.'"

Unlocking his bike, Mason rode the mile or so to the metro station and carried it down the stairs and onto the train. Soon he was downtown, climbing up out of the earth once again, and he locked his wheels to a rack outside the central library. He detoured up the back stairs and through the library's rotunda, passing the grand murals, uplifted just walking through the familiar airy space. He knew generally where the books he wanted were, but he stopped to check the call numbers on his phone before heading into the shelves. There were two definitive works about ley lines in California. He pulled out both and found a free desk to sit and look through them.

Even these ostensibly scholarly tomes offered little of substance about ley lines. One had a large-scale map of the state marked with the most powerful ones, what Steve had called first-order ley lines, one of which cut right through LA County. The other book had a less detailed map of the West and the eastern part of the Pacific, and two of the important lines intersected inland of Los Angeles, but they didn't correspond at all to the position or orientation of the lines in the other book.

Mason sighed and went back to the first one,

Earth Energy Structures of California, to read through the introductory chapter. "Mounting evidence suggests that ley lines and their nodes have shifted position through history," the author explained. "The lines aren't permanent or timeless, instead drifting across the earth, like the ancients' wandering stars in the heavens." Steve had intimated the same idea, but it wasn't encouraging. The book's copyright date was 1963—if the lines did indeed drift, the book's age rendered the maps useless. He checked the other volume, and it was more than a decade older, which explained the discrepancy in the maps.

Pulling his notepad out of his backpack, he made some notes, ignoring the outdated maps and scanning the book for suggestions about locating the lines. Discouraged, he spent some time with the other volume, reading and making notes, but it didn't have any practical advice about locating ley lines and nodes either. Eventually he closed the books and leaned back in his chair, resting his eyes and rolling his neck.

He read through the notes he'd made during his meeting with Matt. Astral projection was an intriguing idea, but Matt had been vague about the details; surely there was a book here to consult about the technique. A quick search of the library's catalog pointed to a couple of texts nearby.

There were several practical guides, including *Astrally Project Your Way to Stock Market Success,* but the one that seemed most promising was *Qigong*

Projection Techniques. He took both books to his desk and started reading. The stock market book outlined the basics of astral projection as Matt had: clear your mind and will yourself to detach from your body. It seemed straightforward. In subsequent chapters there were instructions about tuning in to the buy-and-sell rhythms that the author claimed were inherent in the workings of stock markets, but that wasn't going to help him find ley lines.

The qigong book outlined a very different approach, focusing qi, the fundamental energy that animates living things, to carry your consciousness outside your body so that you could float around and explore higher realms. As he read more, it became clear that the process was essentially the same as the Western version, but couched in Taoist prayers and using qi as the vehicle for projection. It was important to ground yourself first, the book explained, which involved invoking a specific god.

All the procedural minutiae and invocations were easy to disregard, but he wrote some notes about being grounded before starting the projection—that seemed like a good idea. Only adepts who had carefully culti-vated their qi in the correct environment—under the tutelage of a master—should attempt a projection, the text warned, as the deities in other realms were easily angered by unqualified laypeople. That was easy to dismiss too, a symbolic warning in a society where access to powerful tools was closely guarded. In the West, since there was no scientific evidence that astral projection was possible, it was widely dismissed as delusional, making it the province of the few willing to step outside the mainstream. Even though he was taking that step, it didn't mean he was qualified to do it, but hopefully doing the research now would keep him out of danger.

The instructions outlined how to focus your qi through meditation, and once you had sufficiently built it up, how to push the qi through the top of your head, which would carry your conscious mind with it. He made notes about the steps involved, and scanned the rest of the book. Finally, he felt he had a decent understanding of how it was done, in both the East and the West. He closed the texts and slid his notepad into his bag.

On his way out, he noticed a floor plan of the building posted on the wall, and remembered something. He pulled out his phone and did a quick search on where the tarot reference books were shelved: under philosophy, just one flight up, according to the map. Trotting up the staircase, he mused that the philosophy section was an interesting place for the books on tarot, rather than being relegated to the religion section. Clearly the architects of information classification disagreed with Ned on that count.

He soon found the relevant shelves. It was no doubt possible to read all about the tarot online, but it was so hard to navigate through the dross. Even here, in print, there were some questionable resources: *Find Your Soul Mate with the Power of the Tarot,* the racy-sounding *Tarot Sex Magic,* and even *Dr. Wilson's Six-Week Tarot Diet for Optimal Health and Beauty.* After a few minutes he was excited to find *The Practical Tarot Applied to the World We Perceive.* It seemed to relate directly to Anna's recommendation about relating the tarot to his environment. He flipped through it, and it seemed to fit with what she'd told him. He grabbed a general tarot reference guide, with pictures and practical explanations of all the cards, and checked out both books.

Why was he hungry, when he'd just had a big slice of cake? Looking at the time on his phone, though, he realized that had been hours ago. Dinner seemed too far away. He did a quick online search for vegan food trucks—hopefully one would be parked nearby on a Sunday. Sure enough, the vegan hot dog guy and his cart were just a couple of blocks away. He cycled over and bought a dog. He didn't even have to dismount, straddling his bicycle to hand over the cash. Life was good, he thought as he ate—it didn't get much better than cake, gazpacho, and a vegan hot dog all on the same day.

When Mason got home, Peggy and Ned were in the kitchen, Peggy with her long brown hair tied behind her head and an apron over her wiry frame.

"Hey, stranger," he called to her. "You've been gone all weekend."

"It feels like it," she said. "But tonight is all about gazpacho."

"Do you need some help?" he asked, dropping his backpack beside the door.

"You can sit and tell us about your day," Ned said, leaning across the counter to kiss him hello. He was doing something to a cucumber with a knife, and Peggy was deftly dicing tomatoes.

"Sure," Mason said, relieved to be absolved of food prep. "Maybe I'll just squeeze in there and fire up the espresso machine."

"I can do it," Ned said, grinning and setting down his knife. "Park your butt."

Mason climbed onto a stool at the counter. "You missed barley soup last night, Miss Thing," he said. "Wherever you were, it must have been important."

Peggy smiled. "Sorry I missed it. I've been with Andy the last couple of days, scoping out a recording studio. I think it'll work for what I want to do, and it's run by one of his industry friends, so we can use it for cheap."

"That's great news," Mason said. She was working on recording an album, and her brother, Andy, was producing it for her.

"The only limitation is that we have to work there when clients with real money aren't using it," she said. "That means mornings—most bands aren't organized enough to work early in the day."

"That sounds familiar," Ned said, eyeing Mason and switching on the coffee machine.

"I do my best work late," Mason said over the noise, "just like the rock stars. So how are you going to manage it with your job?"

"We go in really early, like four a.m., and work in four-hour blocks. I take my work clothes with me, and I'm in the office by nine."

"You'll be so tired," Mason said. "How long will it take?"

"It depends on how often we can get in there. I'm guessing a month or two. It's nice not to have time constraints."

"As long as you're motivated," Ned said.

"I'm extremely motivated. You guys should come and watch us work one morning. It's early, but it'd be fun."

"I'd love that," Mason said.

Ned murmured agreement and slid a steaming mug of espresso across to him, then went back to his cucumber.

"So I saw my friend Matt today," Mason said, "and it turns out he's single."

"Psychic Matt?" Peggy asked, looking up.

"That's the one."

"I'd be happy to go out with Psychic Matt. Give him my number," Peggy said, scooping tomatoes into the food processor.

"You're brave," Ned said. "I'd want to get his details first."

"I saw him on the news during the whole Billy Blood thing, talking up the science, so I know what he looks like, and how he presents himself," she said. "And if Mason says he's sane …"

"I wouldn't say Mason is exactly an expert on sanity," Ned said.

Mason scowled. "Lucky for us, we have a mental health expert right here."

Peggy flipped on the food processor, shooting him a sweet smile. Mason slid off his stool, not waiting for Ned's retort. Ned had always been clear about his skepticism, but why did he continually have to undermine him? Mason was tired of it. He stretched out on the sofa and got comfortable. Even though the kitchen was just a few yards away, he knew he could ignore the noise and activity enough to try the astral projection techniques he'd read about.

He closed his eyes, tuning out the muted kitchen talk, and cleared his mind, sweeping aside his irritation with Ned and the noise of random thoughts that bubbled up. Breathing deeply, he could feel his body relaxing as well. Matt had said that getting comfortable was the first step. He spent a minute focused on the physical feeling of the couch; the qi book had said he needed to be grounded, and that seemed like a reasonable way to do it, getting a sense of what was underneath him.

The qi book had also gone into detail about building up qi energy, collecting it into a glowing wheel in his abdomen. He tried to visualize a disk of energy, but it didn't feel quite right. Matt and the stock market book had said simply to will his mind to decouple from his body; maybe that would work better.

Detach, he told himself. *Rise up.* He tried to focus on the idea, willing himself to start floating. He drifted into sleep, despite the coffee, overcome by the cumulative energy drain of his day, but he was aware he was asleep, and soon he felt himself rising. He knew his eyes were closed, but he could see the rough white popcorn of the ceiling inching closer. Sunlight streamed in the windows, casting little shadows behind the textured knots of plaster. He focused on them, and knew he was seeing the ceiling up close; it was sharp and clear. He was weightless, floating—it was happening. He thought about the sofa below, and felt a surge of panic at the idea of seeing himself from above. Instantly he crashed back down into his body.

When he opened his eyes, he was still reassuringly sprawled on the sofa. His heart pounded from the rush of adrenaline. It was terrifying to float like that, but exhilarating that he was capable of it. Matt was right: the hard part was going to be managing the fear.

He sat up and rubbed his eyes, breathing deeply to calm down. Ned and Peggy were completely oblivious, still talking gazpacho in the kitchen.

That was enough astral projection, Mason decided. Maybe it would suffuse his subconscious if he set it aside for a while. He rose and grabbed his backpack, then went out to the balcony and cracked open one of the books he'd borrowed, *The Practical Tarot Applied to the World We Perceive.* He scanned the text, reading passages here and there. The concepts aligned with Anna's idea that the symbolism in the cards could be seen in the real world—in places and events, but mostly in people—and thereby provide insight. "Take the Eight of Wands," the author suggested. "The wands race gleefully toward their end, heedless of encumbering circumstances. How many times have you seen friends and associates act this way, rushing toward a goal without due consideration?" Mason opened the other library book, the reference text, and found a picture of the card; sure enough, it depicted eight sticks flying over the countryside. He flipped through the reference book, spending some time reading about the divinatory meanings of the major arcana.

Anna had said something like "the cards are all around you." He could probably find signs of Ned and Peggy in lots of them, but more practically, he wondered about the case he was working on, and Steve. Could he be found in tarot symbolism? More important, could the cards tell him anything about the guy or his quest? He looked back through the major arcana, trying to keep his mind open while he read, expanding his awareness to its edges.

The Tower card caught his eye, but it seemed too dark and dramatic to relate to Steve. The Star was interesting, with its themes of eternity and truth, but it wasn't germane to the matter at hand. The description of the Fool did evoke Steve, in that he seemed cavalier, and his quest was speculative, like the Fool's. There was definitely a parallel with the alchemist in

Steve too, working as a metallurgist, and maybe that also related to his intended purpose for the ley lines. Mason closed his eyes and leaned back, trying to pull more information out of the ether. He saw Steve in his mind's eye, bright-eyed and carefree, and then saw a dark sphere, a globe, crisscrossed with a jumble of fine white lines, like the rubber-band ball Justine had kept on her desk at his old office. But the lines were moving, drifting steadily in all directions, impossible to pin down.

He opened his eyes and sighed. The image didn't seem especially useful right now. He stood up to stretch and leaned on the railing, looking out over their hilly little neighborhood. The sun was still blazing, but low enough in the northwest to be tolerable. He stood there for a minute, enjoying the light. The French doors opened behind him, and before he could turn around, Ned had wrapped his arms around Mason's torso, holding him close.

"Who's my man?" Ned said softly.

"Me."

"You know I don't really think you're crazy, right?"

"I know."

He held on for a moment longer, then pulled away. "So, are you ready to experience the best gazpacho you've ever had in your life?"

Mason laughed, his irritation fading. "Lead the way."

They left the balcony doors open to cool off the house, and ate at the dining table. After the soup,

Ned brought out a crumble he'd made with oats and raspberries from the farmers market.

When Mason crawled into bed later, Ned was already asleep. Mason got comfortable in the dark and tried to form a physical memory of how the bed felt, something to come back to, then told himself to detach from his body and float up. *Be fearless,* he told himself, clearing his mind and willing his consciousness upward, visualizing the qigong disk of energy accumulating and moving toward his head.

He drifted into sleep, and soon became cognizant of the fact that he was dreaming. His suggestion had taken hold: he could see the room around him, in odd shades of dark blue and gray, even though he knew his eyes were closed and it was too dark to see anything. He was rising, he realized, his perspective of the room changing as he floated up into it. Instantly he felt a surge of panic, but he tried to focus beyond the feeling, recalling instead the picture in the qi book of Guanyin, the immortal invoked by astral travelers. The same deity perched on the little table in Anna's front room, he thought dreamily. He looked at the closet door, the chair in the corner, examining their shapes. The panic faded, and when his position remained stable, he willed himself to float higher. *Through the ceiling,* he thought. *Above the house.* The next moment he was looking down on the neighborhood, with no sense of having traveled.

It was a dizzying vantage point, but he focused on the streets and houses so that the fear wouldn't return, driving him back to his bed.

The city didn't look like it did from an airplane at night, or in a drone video. The landscape was in the same monochromatic blues as in his room, with no glare, no bright streetlights, no dark shadows—everything was evenly lit. Even the headlights of the cars winding along the hillside roads cast muted bluish blotches on the street rather than actual light. Overall the effect was surreal, but he was fully aware, and he knew it was real, or at least a version of real—and he was thrilled that he could do this.

He willed himself to move a little higher, and instantly he floated upward, the hills receding and the towers of the financial district coming into view, and far away, lining the horizon, the broad Pacific. The thought of moving caused the movement. As soon as he'd left his room, just the idea of another location shifted him there immediately. *Higher,* he thought, and below him the city flattened out. He was so high that he could see the curvature of the earth, sliding away in all directions. If he fell from this far up … but he pushed that idea aside as quickly as it came, and focused on the arc of the horizon to keep his balance.

The ley lines, he remembered; that was the point of all this. In the wonder of the new experience he'd almost forgotten. *Tune in to the ley lines.* He looked at the city far below, and scanned the horizon. The freeways were visible, and the rivers, all concrete gashes in the landscape, but nothing was perfectly straight, which was the hallmark of ley lines. Gradually, though, at first blue-gray like everything else, then almost white, and glowing—a line appeared, running through the city, as thin as a thread. It disappeared on both horizons, out into the ocean, and east through the mountains into the desert. *That has to be it,* he thought, and reveled in the sight of it for a minute before realizing that he had to try to remember where it was. It cut through a lot of the town, but if he could remember a couple of reference points he could reproduce it.

It was hard to identify the roads and streets. He found the airport, but the white thread was far south of it. The line ran near the loop of freeways around downtown, and scanning the area he found the Coliseum, where the thread grazed one corner. He could remember that: the Coliseum. He followed the line east-northeast, past downtown, looking for landmarks along its length. It crossed a riverbed right at the foot of the mountains. A freeway ran alongside the river, but where was that, exactly? There were scars in the earth all around, pits—quarries, he realized, which meant that had to be the 605, where it ended.

Remember, he told himself, concentrating on the landmarks. But was he forgetting something? Lost in thought, he wondered idly what it would look like if he went even higher up, how far he'd be able to see the luminous thread stretching out, and in that moment he accelerated upward. "Stop," he shouted, suddenly terrified of getting blown out into space, losing not just his body but his whole planet.

With that, he was plunged into darkness, the beautiful white thread and the landscape gone. It took him a moment to get his bearings, still breathing hard from the moment of fear. He couldn't see anything, but he was back, grounded, in his own body—he could feel it—and in his own bed, the familiar dim clock on Ned's cell phone glowing in the dark.

He thought about it for a minute, slowly calming down. It had definitely happened. It was far too vivid to have been a dream. And he'd found what he was looking for. He grinned in the dark. Matt had been right—astral projection was an excellent technique for this case.

He quietly got out of bed and went into the office, closing the door behind him. He wanted to write down the clues he'd gathered so he wouldn't lose them overnight. He rolled his shoulders to get the blood moving, then pulled out his notepad, but before he started to write he had a better idea. He pulled open his computer and found a site where he could make a customized map, then zoomed in on the city to locate the Coliseum, and the end of the 605. He drew a line between them, adjusting it to reflect exactly where he'd seen the luminous thread from above, then zoomed out and extended the line, out into the ocean and up into the mountains. He stared at it for a few moments. It looked right, based on what he'd seen.

Then he realized what he'd missed—Steve was after a node, not just a line. How had he forgotten that? The projection experience had been an altered state of consciousness, he decided—dreamlike, even though he'd been lucid enough to reproduce what he'd seen.

He'd find the node, though; he'd found this much already. But not tonight. His skin felt like it was buzzing from the experience, and it was going to be hard to sleep. He saved the map and closed his computer, then carefully climbed back into bed, shifting closer to Ned and wrapping an arm around him. Ned stirred but didn't wake. As he'd feared, it took Mason a long time to get back to sleep.

THREE

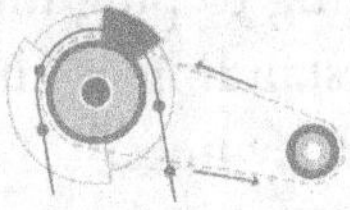

After slurping down most of a mug of espresso, sitting out on the balcony with his eyes half closed and warming up to the day, Mason was lucid enough to go into the office. Ned was at his desk, peering at his computer and engrossed in a work phone call, but he looked up and winked at Mason when he came in. Mason flipped open his computer and pulled up the map he'd made the night before, trying to tune out Ned's conversation. Seeing it on the screen, the line looked so decisive. The feeling of floating over the city had been surreal, dreamy, but this was unequivocal—real-world information pulled from an extrasensory experience.

It was too hard to focus with Ned's mortgage talk,

so he picked up his computer and went back to the balcony, got comfortable in a chair, and made his own phone call. Steve picked up after a couple of rings.

"I did some preliminary research," Mason said, "and I'm pretty sure I'll be able to help you."

"That's great news," Steve said, so loud that Mason had to pull the phone away from his ear. "Did you find the power point?"

"Uh … do you mean the supernode?" Mason asked, frowning.

"Right—the supernode. Same thing."

"Are you planning to plug into it or something? Because my understanding is that you can't really harvest energy from ley lines."

"I'm glad you're willing to take on the work," Steve said, sounding guarded now. "We should probably discuss a timeline."

"I don't think it'll take long at all—maybe a day or two. I've made a good start." He wasn't completely sure he'd be able to find it, but it wasn't bluster to say that he could. He believed it, felt it.

"And what about a budget?"

"I was thinking a grand for the precise location of the supernode."

"That sounds fine," Steve said. "There will probably be more work later on, but we can start with that. Do you want me to pay you up front?"

"No—Justine vouches for you, that's all I need."

"And if I stiff you, you know where she lives," Steve said.

Mason laughed. "I'll let you know when I have more info for you," he said, and ended the call.

More work later, he'd said—what else could possibly be involved? More concerning was how he'd dodged the question about what he was going to do with the information. Matt's comment about nefarious intent ran through his mind. In a way, it was none of Mason's business why the guy wanted to find the supernode—but he didn't want to aid in any misdoing either. There was nothing about Steve that seemed hinky, though, and if there were, Mason's intuition surely would have picked it up by now.

He sat for a while, lost in thought. If the lines were essentially inert, how could they be used in any way, destructive or otherwise? The authorities on the matter didn't even agree as to whether they had any impact on human activity. He pulled open his laptop and spent a couple of hours wading through more on the subject, looking for evidence that the lines could be exploited. Everything written about them was vague, however, and only implied that positive things came from the energy involved.

When it got too warm on the balcony, he closed his computer and went inside to look in on Ned.

"You must be starved," Mason said, setting his computer down on his desk.

Ned smiled. "I had lunch when you were having your morning coffee. I'm going downtown for a meeting in a few minutes, but I could make you a sandwich first."

"Not if you're not eating. I'll fend for myself."

"There are some leftovers, and Peggy will be home for dinner, so we'll make something fun." Ned kissed him good-bye and headed out.

Mason found the leftovers in the fridge and sat at the counter, eating directly out of the containers, not bothering to heat anything up. It was nice to have the house to himself, and he spent a minute enjoying the quiet.

But there was work to do. He made another pot of espresso and stretched out on the sofa. It took a minute to get completely comfortable, but once he was, he started the process for astral projection: first getting grounded, then telling himself to detach. It didn't take him long to drift into the hypnagogic state, despite the bright daylight streaming in the windows and the amount of caffeine coursing through his veins. Disjointed images ran through his mind: Anna's bright neon window sign, Guanyin, the Star card from the tarot deck. *Detach,* he thought, willing himself to rise out of his body.

He was more aware of it happening this time, and felt the flash of fear sooner too, but by concentrating on what he was seeing he managed to stabilize the experience. *The ley lines,* he told himself, and instantly he was back above the city, not blue this time but green and gray, still surreal but lit by daylight. It was still there, the perfect white thread running through the landscape, under the 605 and the river, under all the freeways and all the rivers. *Where are the other ones?*

he asked himself. That was the only way he could find a node, by finding more than one thread.

But then he realized there were others, just not as bright as the first one. Had they been there all along? He focused more intently, and more of them appeared, right at the threshold of his perception. But as he looked at them, they became clearer, and more lines, even fainter, appeared between them, crisscrossing the land. It was like watching the sky at night; the longer you looked, the more stars you could see. Maybe this world really was a rubber-band ball. Maybe everything was made of lines, smaller and fainter until there was nothing else. He averted his attention. It was too much to think about.

The bright lines—that was what Steve had said. Look for the bright lines. And there was one, not as bright as the first one he'd perceived, but brighter than the rest. It ran almost north-south, from the Valley toward the harbor. Landmarks, he thought. He needed reference points to be able to reproduce it. The thread crossed the coastline near the harbor, not near a significant point, but then it went directly under a pyramid. He knew that place; it was on a college campus. *Remember the pyramid,* he told himself. He followed the glowing thread north, and found another landmark near the tangle of freeways downtown, where it crossed one end of the Cornfield. That should be easy to remember too, the amoeba-shaped park at the edge of Chinatown.

The node. Find the node. He followed the new

thread back to where it crossed the brighter one, and focused on the point of intersection, which caused him to float lower. The threads crossed under the worn grass in someone's backyard, in a dense little neighborhood near the snarl of freeways that dissected Boyle Heights. He focused on the yard, floating lower over the houses. There was a third line there, he realized, just as Steve had said, crossing exactly the same point that the other two did, fainter than the others but definitely there, creating a lopsided asterisk.

He didn't know the streets around here, but he could find the node again if he could remember landmarks. He looked at the cramped backyards, the roofs. The node was in a yard next door to the only house on the block with a Spanish-tile roof— that would help narrow it down. It felt like a lot to remember, but he tried to store it. He got closer to the ground, admiring the white threads under the lawn. No matter how close he got, they were never more than hair-thin. Beautiful, inert, like jewelry—he could stare at them for ages. But something nagged at the edge of his mind, and he knew he shouldn't linger.

Go back, he told himself, and the aerial view was gone. His eyes were closed, safely back in his own skin, grounded, back on the sofa. He blinked, coming to full consciousness. That had been real, even though it felt dreamy. He dragged himself up off the sofa and went to his computer, where he pulled up his map to add the new line.

It was easy to find the pyramid, but the Cornfield

was harder. It didn't look quite the same on the computer, and the thread he'd seen hadn't touched a specific marker there, just one end of the field. He drew the line where he thought it had been, then scrolled back to where it intersected the one he'd found the night before. The point where the lines crossed was in the middle of a street, but that wasn't right; it had been in a backyard, he remembered that. What else? The images were fading, the way dreams faded, and he had to concentrate to pull them back. Spanish tile, he remembered. It wasn't far away, the only house with a tile roof in the satellite image, and he nudged the new line until the node was in the right place, under the ratty grass. He zoomed out, and saw that the line still ran under the far end of the Cornfield; this had to be right.

There had been a third line, but he didn't have reference points for it. It didn't really matter, he decided, since it was there, intersecting the others. He clicked on the point where the lines crossed and got the latitude and longitude numbers, copying them into an email draft. He wasn't going to send it just yet, though; he didn't want Steve to think he hadn't had to work hard for it. That was the easiest thousand bucks he'd ever made, he thought, smiling to himself and folding his computer closed.

As promised, Peggy was home for dinner. Ned made lentil burgers with caramelized onions and a tahini sauce. Ned put everything on the dining table, and before he sat down Mason propped opened the French doors, partly to cool off the house and partly to clear out the strong smell of well-cooked onions.

"How's your earth lines research going?" Peggy asked him, assembling a burger.

"I think I'm done," he said. "I found the node that the guy asked me to find."

"That's great news," she said. "How did you do it?"

He glanced at Ned, who was spooning onions onto his plate. He shared more of the out-there stuff with Peggy than with Ned, but he didn't want to have to censor himself. "Astral projection," he said.

"When did you learn to do that?" Ned asked.

"From Matt the other day, and from some library books."

"How does it work?" Peggy asked.

He explained it in general terms, but didn't get into the bizarre otherworldly feeling of the experience.

"And you learned it from books?" Ned said, forcing a smile.

At least he was trying not to sound judgmental, Mason thought. "Yeah—there's even a qigong approach, although you're supposed to invoke the goddess 108 times, but who has time for that? I kind of combined all the techniques, and it worked."

"So you can see things when you're floating around," Ned said, "but obviously not with your eyes—they're still on the ground."

"I guess I'm seeing things with my mind. The

experience is kind of surreal, like watching an immersive video rather than actually flying over the city."

"Interesting," Ned said. He asked Peggy, "Had you ever heard of ley lines before?"

"No, but I'm curious why the client guy wants to find them."

"I'm wondering about that too," Mason said. "I'm going to call him tomorrow, so maybe I'll ask."

"If you could do anything with them," Ned said, "don't you think they'd have been exploited by now? There are ten million people living around here. Wouldn't somebody have dug them up and strip-mined them or something?"

"None of the written sources indicate that they're exploitable," Mason said. "They're just kind of there."

"Or," Ned said carefully, "maybe they're not exploited because they don't exist."

Mason swallowed his anger. "They do exist, because I've seen them," he said, as calmly as possible, setting his burger down. "And beyond my own experience, any scientist would accept that not everything that exists has been found yet. That's why they build particle accelerators and launch space probes."

"I don't think any scientists are out there looking for ley lines, though," Ned said. "It seems so … woo-woo."

"You know he's right, Nedly," Peggy said, grinning at him. "Just say it."

"Hmm," Ned said, and bit into his burger.

"Say it," she insisted.

"OK," Ned said, wiping his mouth with his napkin and leaning back in his chair, eyeing Mason. "I concede that not everything that exists has been found yet."

"There you go," Mason said. "How hard was that?"

"Like the 101 at rush hour," Peggy said grimly.

Ned laughed, and got up to bring the fruit salad he'd made from the kitchen.

He was still feeling warm about Ned, basking in the absence of irritation, when he climbed into bed. He shifted close to him, nuzzling his neck, massaging the soles of Ned's feet with his toes, wordlessly pressing him to connect.

"Somebody's randy," Ned said, grinning at him and putting his book on the nightstand. He rolled up, straddling Mason, running his hands over his chest.

Sinking into unconsciousness, in that warm, comfortable frame of mind after they'd had sex, Mason gave himself the suggestion to remember his dreams. He soon found himself walking on a busy street, somewhere crowded, maybe downtown. The other people walking around seemed gray, washed-out, flat. He felt himself experiencing the dream but didn't try to manipulate it, instead peering at the faces as they drifted past. But there was nothing to see—he couldn't register the details or pull out any feeling, any connection. Maybe they weren't actually people, he realized. It was a disturbing thought, and he pushed himself to swim up out of sleep. He took the yellow pad out of the nightstand and scribbled down what he could remember: "Lifeless people. Colorless faces. Two-dimensional."

FOUR

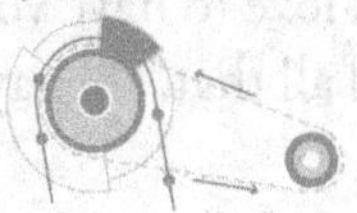

Mason knew himself well enough not to make any major decisions before he'd ingested a couple of cups of coffee, but by the time he'd had some fruit for breakfast and was fully awake, he had decided it was time to wrap things up with Steve. He went in and sat at his desk, greeted Ned, who was absorbed in his computer screen, and started an email. He included the coordinates of the node, and a link to the map he'd made with the two lines drawn on it. He ended with his own street address so Steve could send him a check.

He was still at his desk reading emails a few minutes later when his phone rang. He pulled it out and looked at the caller ID: "Steve Glaser."

"Hey, Steve," he answered, and went out to the balcony so as not to disturb Ned.

"You did it," Steve said. "You figured it out."

"It took a bit of research," Mason said, leaning on the balcony railing, "but once I was able to tune in, it was pretty clear."

"Do you have some time today to drive out there with me?"

"Uh … do you need me to be there? The map shows exactly where it is."

"The map is just the beginning, Mason. I'm sure it's accurate, but I'd love to have you along, to double-check the vibes and all that. I'll pay you your day rate, of course."

He would have preferred to just be done with it and get paid, but he remembered that Steve had warned him there might be more to do. Going along for the ride might also reveal more about what Steve was going to do with the info.

"I guess I can do that," Mason said. "Do you want to meet there later?"

"I'll pick you up. You're kind of on the way, if I take the 134. I'll be there in thirty minutes."

Half an hour gave Mason just enough time to put on a decent shirt and have another coffee, and then his phone chimed with a text from Steve: "I'm outside."

He kissed Ned good-bye and pulled on his backpack. Out front he found a classic car—from the eighties, he guessed, its big old motor idling audibly—with the windows rolled down and Steve behind the wheel. He was wearing a summery plaid shirt, and greeted Mason like an old friend.

"Sweet ride," Mason said as he climbed in, fumbling with the unfamiliar old-school seatbelt. "What is it, exactly?"

"It's a Delta Eighty-Eight," Steve said, shifting into gear and deftly aiming the vehicle down the hill toward the boulevard.

"I love it." Mason admired the nearly unmarred wood-paneled dashboard, the spindly steering wheel. "My boyfriend has two classic cars, a Barracuda and a big old Crown Vic."

"I used to drive a newer car, a Beamer, but you know what they say about Jewish guys driving German cars."

Mason didn't know, but said, "Sure." Steve accelerated up the ramp onto the freeway. "So what year is it? I know Ned will ask."

"It's an '82 coupe."

Mason made a mental note of that and looked in the backseat, admiring the spaciousness. Incongruous with the immaculate upholstery was a cardboard box behind Steve's seat, spilling over with a jumble of plastic and metal tubing, wires, and machine parts.

"I hope that stuff didn't come out of the engine," he said, raising his voice to be heard over the road noise.

"It's actually going into the engine, once I get it working," he said, not taking his eyes off the road.

He drove confidently and fast.

"Is it for smog control?" Mason asked.

"It's a device that will increase my gas mileage a hundredfold," he said. "Imagine driving to Albuquerque and back on four dollars' worth of gas."

"Really? How does it work?"

"It's about aerating the fuel and getting the right kind of turbulence in the fuel line. I haven't figured out the physics, exactly, but a bunch of people have built them at home, and I'm working on one. We share information online—a virtual community of tinkerers."

"Other people actually got it working?"

"Lots of them. I will too, at some point. It's actually easier to install them on cars of this vintage—new cars have way too much electronics."

"If someone got it working, why wouldn't they sell it to GM or Toyota?" Mason asked.

"Because they collude with the oil companies, so they can all keep selling their products. They're happy with the status quo—our addiction to oil. Anything that would disrupt their profits gets suppressed."

Mason looked back at the box again. The guy was a scientist, but it looked more like a plumber's junk drawer than a revolutionary new technology. One of Ned's good friends, Gilbert, was into conspiracy theories. Mason had always dismissed him as a wide-eyed believer, but several of the outlandish things Gilbert had told him later turned out to be true, and had helped him solve a couple of different cases. And Mason was learning that the deeper he dove into his own psychic experiences, the stranger things got. He couldn't dismiss anything out of hand anymore.

"I hope you can get it working," he said.

Steve kept his eyes on the traffic. "I'll figure it out. I've got a lot on my plate right now."

"Like ley lines."

"Exactly," Steve said, his tone brightening. "So how did you locate the supernode, anyway? I'm impressed that you found it so fast."

"One of the techniques we psychics employ is astral projection," Mason said, and briefly explained soaring above the city to find the glowing strands.

"Do you do that a lot?"

"It's one of the techniques in my repertoire," Mason said.

They exited the freeway and stopped at the traffic light at the bottom of the ramp. He had been in this neighborhood before, Boyle Heights or close to it, but not very often. It was residential but felt claustrophobic, small Victorian houses packed tightly together on narrow lots.

"My grandparents used to live around here," Steve said.

"Really? It's pretty Latino these days."

"Things change." He turned a corner and slowed to a crawl. "It's this street, isn't it? Your map shows the node behind the third house from the corner."

"That sounds right. It looked different from

overhead." He leaned forward, craning to see the rooftops. "You're right, it's behind that house—the one next door has the Spanish tile."

"Excellent," Steve said, and accelerated down the block. "I don't want to park out front," he explained. "This car draws enough attention as it is."

They parked and climbed out, Mason pausing to stretch his back.

"Come on," Steve said, and set off at a determined gait back toward the house. Mason caught up with him.

The house was obviously occupied, with curtains and a floor lamp visible through the front window, a kid's tricycle on the porch. Steve slowed his pace and looked the place over, but didn't stop.

"Lucky for us, there's an alley," he said. Mason followed him around the corner, where the alley's ancient potholed pavement connected with the side street. It was lined with garage doors and walls. Some of them were too high to see over, but the third house had a simple chain-link fence, granting them a good view.

"This is it, right?" Steve said, excitement in his voice.

"It looks like it," Mason said, surveying the yard. The home had a single-car garage on the alley, but beside it was a tatty lawn, with a set of chairs and a barbecue up near the house. "I remember the patchy grass."

"Is there any way you can tune in now, to be sure

it's there?" Steve looked at him expectantly. "I mean, can you point it out to me?"

"I guess so," Mason said. It made him nervous to be looking into someone's yard, like a burglar casing the joint, and it was annoying to be asked to verify it when he was certain this was the right yard. But he was getting paid to be here, and maybe it wouldn't hurt to double-check. "Give me a minute."

He'd learned a direction-finding technique recently on a case involving an NSA operative. He'd used it to find her, and it was effective for locating missing objects too, so it might work now. The node point was in this yard; with a little concentration perhaps he could point to the precise spot.

Steve moved a few feet away, giving him space to work. Mason closed his eyes and cleared his thoughts, pushing aside the random chatter, until his conscious mind was quiet and empty. He thought about how the shimmering lines had looked from his psychic vantage point, crossing in the earth below him. He expanded his awareness to the edges of his mind, open to any insight that might come. At first, nothing seemed to drift in. *You're good at this,* he reminded himself. Before long he felt the node pulling his mind toward it, drawing him in, its position unambiguous. Even with his eyes closed, he could have pointed to it. He couldn't walk over to it, because of the fence, but when he opened his eyes he could pinpoint the spot in the scrubby grass.

He chuckled and looked at Steve.

"What's funny?"

"Nothing. I'm just happy that I found it—again. It's a bit of a rush to have it confirmed when I'm standing right in front of it."

Steve's eyes grew wide. "Where is it?"

"Right there." Mason pointed to the spot on the lawn. "It's halfway between the end of the garage and the house, then about ten feet in from the fence, and down in the earth."

Steve stood looking at the mottled dirt and grass for a minute, hands on his hips. "So this is it," he said quietly.

"Now that you know where it is, what are you going to do with it?"

"Nothing yet," he said, pulling his eyes away from the lawn to look at Mason. "It's under someone's yard. I'm just glad it's not in the middle of a street."

"Why? Are you going to dig it up?"

Steve frowned. "It's not about me, Mason. The energy structure here benefits the whole city. I'm sure two hundred years ago it was closer to the Pueblo, or downtown, and that's why all that stuff is where it is. But today it's right here."

That didn't really answer his question, so Mason tried another angle. "Too bad it's not for sale," he said. "Then you could do whatever you want with it."

"There were a couple of other real estate signs on the block, though. Maybe I can work something out."

At that moment a young woman in a sweatshirt

stepped out the back door of the house.

"Can I help you?" she said sharply. Mason felt his heart start pounding.

"Hi," Steve called to her, smiling broadly. "I'm just admiring your place. I grew up in this house, and I was driving by, so I thought I'd show it to my nephew here."

"OK," the woman said, folding her arms.

"I used to ride my tricycle around in this yard," he continued.

"I've only been here a couple of years," she said warily.

"I see," he said. "Well, we won't take any more of your time. I'm glad someone is taking care of the place." He raised his hand in a nonchalant wave and turned, leisurely walking up the alley, back toward the side street. Mason nodded to the homeowner and followed Steve.

"A young family in a small house," Steve said. "That might work."

"Work for what?" Mason asked as they stepped back out onto the side street.

"When we walk past the front of the house," Steve said, ignoring the question, "don't stop walking, but look over and nod, as if I'm telling you all about it. If there's anyone looking out the windows, wave at them, but don't stop walking."

Mason did as instructed, amused by Steve's effortless subterfuge.

"There's no one watching," Steve said quietly

as they walked by. "That's very good; it means she believed me."

"We could have asked her to let us into the yard," Mason said.

"No need. Besides, no one would believe the real reason we're here—she'd tell everyone in the neighborhood. 'This crazy guy is obsessed with my backyard.' No, it's better not to attract attention."

"I guess that makes sense," Mason said. "So are you going to try to get in there?" He wasn't sure he would believe the answer anyway. Steve was obviously an expert at dodging the truth.

"I'm not going to sneak in there," he said, frowning. "Give me some credit. I'm going to buy the place."

"OK," Mason said, looking at him carefully.

They were at the car, and as they climbed in, Steve turned to Mason, concern in his eyes. "I probably should have mentioned it sooner, but you'll have to keep all of this to yourself."

"You mean the location of the node?"

"Exactly. If the owners think I want it for nostalgic reasons, it'll be cheaper than if they think there's something valuable buried in the yard."

"Fair enough," Mason said. "I'll keep my mouth shut."

"Good," Steve said. He grinned at Mason, then reached for the ignition key and started the engine.

Back on the freeway, Steve seemed happier, Mason thought. He drove more slowly and seemed more relaxed, maybe relieved.

"You've been incredibly helpful with all of this," Steve said as he pulled up in front of Mason's place. "I'll cut you a check later this week."

"I'm glad I could help," he said, climbing out and gently pushing the heavy car door closed.

"We're not done yet, Mason. I'll need you out there again once I have the property."

"Sure—I'm around," Mason said, and watched the sleek old car drive away.

The house was empty when he went inside. He checked his phone for messages, and Ned had texted:

> Going to an AA meeting. Eating out with the gang after.

He was sitting out on the balcony enjoying the late-afternoon sun when he heard Peggy get home from work.

"Are you in for dinner?" he asked, going inside to greet her.

"I am," she said, stooping to take off her shoes. "And lucky for you, I didn't get up early to go to the studio today, so I have the energy to cook. If there's garlic, I'll make that Caesar salad."

"I'll check," Mason said, and went into the kitchen. "Victory," he called to her a moment later. "There's a whole bulb."

"Let me get changed and wind down, then we can work on it. You have to wash the lettuce."

"Deal," Mason said.

Over dinner he told her about his outing with

Steve, and she told him about her plans for the upcoming recording sessions. It felt good to talk to her—she was motivated to be productive with the studio time, and her enthusiasm was contagious.

Ned was upbeat too when he got home, buoyed by the fellowship at his meeting. Mason gave him the abridged version of his trip with Steve, and later, in bed, Ned got him laughing by relating the antics of one of his AA friends. He loved this, the times when they were effortlessly connected, agreeing on everything.

His time in the dream world was less positive. He didn't come to awareness to maneuver in the dream, despite trying to. He was somewhere dark, and an amorphous mass of aggression swelled around, intimidating him. He struggled to fend it off, fought not to be overwhelmed. At one point it was pressing down on his chest, and he struggled to breathe. He woke up, gulping air, propelled into consciousness by fear. Deciding not to bother to write down the details—it seemed too nonspecific—he instead spent a few minutes clearing his mind, consciously redirecting his thoughts to prevent a return to that ugliness, before drifting off again.

In the light of morning he was able to forget about the dream. He pulled on a T-shirt and a pair of boxer shorts and went to the kitchen, starting up the espresso machine and yawning. The room was already redolent with the smell of strong coffee, he realized, and noticed the *briki* pot on the stove.

Ned came out of the office, dressed for a day working at home. "Gilbert's coming over for coffee," he said. "You might want to put some pants on."

Mason went back to their bedroom to pull on a pair of cargo shorts. Gilbert was a lifelong friend of Ned's, and had a knack for making Mason uncomfortable. Mason had introduced him to a woman he knew from the library, and they had hit it off, but still, something in Gilbert's manner always felt wanton.

He heard the doorbell ring and walked back down the hall. Ned let Gilbert in, and went into the kitchen to pour the coffee.

"Look at you," Gilbert said, pulling Mason into a tight hug, planting his lips on his neck, his palm sliding into the small of his back. "You look great." He held on for some time after Mason let go. Mason decided it would be more awkward to pull away. Gilbert was probably just expressing the kinship they had developed out in the desert, when Mason had helped him sort out his father's estate.

"Thanks," Mason said, once he was finally free. "Come and sit."

Gilbert sat in the middle of the sofa, and Mason took an easy chair. Ned came in with demitasse cups for the three of them and sat with Gilbert.

"Greek style," he said, sliding a cup across the coffee table toward Mason. "Gilbert's is the one with four sugars."

"You know what I like," Gilbert said, picking up his cup.

Mason sipped the coffee, enjoying the bit of grit that came up when he swirled the cup. Ned only made Greek coffee when Gilbert was around, as it was Gilbert's preferred method of imbibing caffeine, so it was a treat.

"You have remarkable calf muscles," Gilbert said, his gaze lingering on Mason's legs. "It must be all that cycling."

"Thanks," he said, crossing his legs and wishing he'd put on long pants. "How's your girlfriend?" he asked pointedly.

"She's great. Working hard."

"Have you ever heard of a homemade device that improves your gas mileage when you attach it to your car's engine?" he asked.

"Sure. You have to build it yourself, though, because whenever somebody tries to market one, the oil companies shut them down."

"I thought those didn't really work," Ned said, sipping from his cup.

"That's what they want you to think," Gilbert said, his eyes growing wide. "When you debunk something with the voice of authority and the weight of corporate money behind it, people just accept it."

"Not you, though," Mason said.

"Of course not. I can see through their subterfuge."

"Why are you worried about fuel-saving devices?"

Ned asked Mason. "You don't even have a car."

"My client had a box of parts in his backseat, and he said he was building one. He actually said the same thing, that it's being suppressed by big oil and the automakers."

"He's right," Gilbert said. "If he gets it working, let me know—I'll get him to build one for me."

FIVE

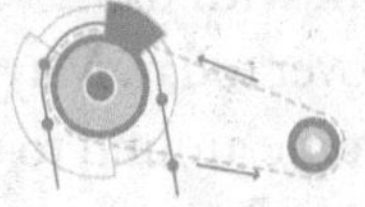

Steve had promised there'd be more to do, and a couple of months later, toward the end of summer, Mason heard from him again. The ringing woke him, pulling him up into semi-consciousness. He always set his phone so it wouldn't bother him until nine, which was early for Mason, but the rest of the world had some messed-up ideas about when business was to be conducted.

"Braithwaite," he mumbled, blinking the sleep out of his eyes.

"Sorry to wake you," the familiar voice said.

"Oh, I wasn't sleeping," Mason said, struggling to speak clearly. "So did you buy that house?"

"I did—it wasn't a cake walk, but I made it

happen."

"Congrats," Mason said sleepily.

"Are you available to do some work? Now that I've taken possession, I'd like you to come and locate the node for me again. It won't have moved very much since you were here, but I need a precise location for it."

"I'm sure I'll be able to help with that."

"Can I pay you your day rate?"

"That suits me," he said. "When do you want me to come by?"

"Soon. Today, if you can make it. I'll hire some day laborers to work with us."

"I could come over today. Maybe early afternoon."

"I'll be here. Come around to the back—I'll be in the yard or the garage."

Mason pulled himself up out of bed and went to the kitchen. The house was quiet. Ned had probably gone for lunch at his parents' place; his mother often cooked for the family after mass on Sunday. Mason had a standing invitation but usually wasn't functional in time. He made coffee and ate some nectarines and a pear, figuring out how to get to Steve's house on public transit.

After his second pot of espresso he was clear-headed enough to pull on his backpack and jump on his bicycle. He coasted down the hill to the metro station, changed trains downtown, and soon disembarked in Steve's new neighborhood, cycling the quiet side streets, working up a little sweat in the heat of the day.

Pulling up, he saw that the Delta Eighty-Eight was parked on the street out front. Maybe Steve was using the garage for some higher purpose. The house looked the same as before, although the curtains were drawn, and there was none of the usual debris of daily life in the tiny fenced-in front yard or on the porch. The latch on the iron gate was unlocked when he tried it, so he pushed his bike inside, parking it out of view in the narrow space beside the house, and then walked the rest of the way through to the backyard.

It looked like a construction site. Gone were the lawn chairs and the barbecue. Back by the alley was a peaked white canopy, the kind people use as a sunshade for a party in the park. It hadn't been set up yet, its support poles and anchors piled beside it. More intriguing was a haphazard collection of metal parts spread out on the lawn: lengths of narrow pipe, some curved, some angled, some quite long; a gleaming stainless-steel cone, about three feet tall; and a pair of flat half-moons made of thick sheet metal. He couldn't imagine what it was all for.

Back near the garage were a couple of guys dressed for manual labor, both of them wielding shovels. As he got closer he saw that they were digging a shallow trench out from the side of the garage. One of them looked up at Mason as he walked over.

"I'm looking for Steve," he said.

"*¡Patrón!*" the man called toward the garage, and Steve soon appeared from the back door, wearing baggy jeans and a dirt-smudged T-shirt.

"You made it," he said, a broad grin on his face. "Did you meet the guys?"

"Not yet."

He introduced them as Flaco, tall and thin but well-muscled, and Gabe, who was a little older. They greeted Mason and then went back to their shovels.

"We went ahead and got started," Steve explained. "We're digging a trench for the electrical wiring right now."

"So what's all this stuff?" Mason asked, looking around the yard.

"That," he said, pointing at the array of steel components, "is the machine I built. You know I'm a metallurgist by trade, right? While I was working on acquiring the house, I designed it and had a machinist fabricate it. You're going to help me position it today."

Mason looked at the jumble of pieces, trying to imagine what it would look like assembled. "Is it to harness the energy of the ley lines?"

"No," he said slowly, his eyes growing wide. "It's to energize them."

"You're going to pump electricity into them? What will that do?"

"Not electricity," he said impatiently, as if talking to a kid. "What it'll do is improve everyone's quality of life. The beneficial effects will be immeasurable, radiating for miles around."

Mason frowned. "What kind of effects?"

"Good vibes for everyone—prosperity, for

example, and more clarity and intensity in people's emotional states."

"Hey, *patrón*," Gabe called, and Steve went over to where they were digging. They had uncovered a buried iron pipe crossing the trench, and the three of them spent a few minutes discussing what to do with it.

Mason took the time to assess what was going on. He'd assumed all along that Steve wanted to locate the node to use it for personal gain, but this was something different. The divergent theories on ley lines were that they either attracted human activity or resulted from it, but Mason hadn't found anything about manipulating them. He felt relieved that Steve wasn't going to use them as Matt had suggested, to rob banks or blow things up. But it was a big investment of time and money for what sounded like a vague goal. There had to be more to it.

"It's an old irrigation pipe," Steve said, returning. "The guys are going to get a saw from my truck to take it out." As they spoke, Flaco walked through the gate in the chain-link fence and started rummaging in the back of a white half-ton parked just outside in the alley. "In the meantime, maybe you and I can work on locating the node." He tapped his temple knowingly.

"Sure," Mason said. "Can you give me some space?"

"I'll go get a flag," Steve said, and went into the garage.

The direction-finding technique had worked well before, so Mason decided to use it again. He took off his backpack and set it on the ground, then walked over to the part of the yard where the node had been. Closing his eyes, he worked to quiet his thoughts, then recalled the view he'd had from above in the astral projection, the glowing threads intersecting in the earth. He shifted focus to the periphery, anticipating the information bleeding into his awareness. It took a few minutes of concentrating, but eventually he felt the node point, in the earth, a few feet away. He turned toward it, eyes still closed, and stepped closer, until it was almost directly below him. It was an unmistakable signal, he realized, not a physical sensation but visible in his mind's eye. The threads stretched away beneath his feet, he could feel them— perfectly straight, east and west, north and south, rooted but powerful. The sensation was like standing on a glass floor, with the line clearly exposed in the space below.

He dropped to his knees and put his hands on the dirt, then opened his eyes and said, "Ha!" grinning to himself at the success. The threads were so clear, so tangible, shimmering down there. When he looked up, Steve was standing a few yards away, by the garage, watching him intently. Flaco was staring at him too, eyes wide, the power saw dangling forgotten in his hand, its electric cord trailing in the dirt. He said something in Spanish, and Gabe looked up from his shovel work in surprise; the only word Mason understood was *brujo*. He knew what it meant, "sorcerer" or "witch," but he couldn't tell whether Flaco was intrigued or fearful.

"I'm not a *brujo*," Mason said firmly, looking him in the eye. Flaco nodded but didn't look entirely convinced.

"Have you found it?" Steve asked.

"It's right here." He patted the dirt with his palms.

He walked over quickly and knelt beside Mason. "Between your hands?"

"Just between my fingertips. It's down in the earth, but this is the point."

Steve dropped to one knee and pushed the length of stiff wire that he was holding into the earth between Mason's fingers, then sat back on his haunches, staring at the yellow plastic ribbon tied to the marker. Mason pulled his hands away and sat back too.

"This has been a long time coming," Steve said finally.

Mason wanted to ask more about why and how he was going to energize the node, but there was an intense, faraway look in Steve's eyes. Not lifting his gaze from the little wire flag, Steve leaned forward, onto his knees, and put his hands around it, then lay flat on the grass, prostrate, as if in prayer.

Harmless, Mason reminded himself. Justine had promised he was eccentric, but harmless.

Steve sat up again at the sudden shriek of high-speed metal on metal; Flaco had gotten the power saw working.

Mason got to his feet, and once they'd finished cutting out the length of pipe and the saw was quiet, he said to Steve, "I guess you're done with me?"

"Have you got somewhere you need to be?" he asked, his eyes narrowing. "Stick around for a while. This won't take long, and I want you to see it when it's finished."

"I am curious," Mason admitted, and after all, he was getting paid. "I'd be happy to stay."

Steve turned to Gabe and Flaco. "Let's go," he said, and in a muddle of English and broken Spanish he told them what he wanted done at the flag. Mason sat cross-legged a few yards away on a patch of dead grass, watching them work. They drove three metal posts into the earth, spaced evenly around the flag, and then started bolting on lengths of pipe. In half an hour the device had started to take shape—a steel ring of pipe several feet across, suspended a few inches above the ground, and in the center they mounted the steel cone, inverted so that it pointed directly down toward the node, its wide base open to the sky.

"Can you help me carry the motor?" Steve asked him.

Mason got to his feet and followed him into the garage. One wall was hung with dozens of tools, some of them familiar and some arcane, made for precision work. The workbench was cluttered, but there was room to park a vehicle inside. The electrical breaker box, mounted near the door to the yard, looked brand-new.

"Did you put that in for an electric car?" Mason asked.

"No. I wanted high voltage for the machine—just in case."

Mason was about to ask what the machine was going to do with all that power when Steve said, "Here it is."

On the workbench sat an intricate-looking electrical device, vaguely oblong, sprouting wires and gears.

"You take the end with the gearbox," Steve said.

It was heavy, but not unmanageable. Steve walked backward, looking over his shoulder as he made his way, grunting with the effort. Mason's mind flashed to the tarot books, and remembered the character who walked backward—the Fool. Walking backward symbolized not being aware of things that might lead to your downfall. Could that apply to Steve, building this bizarre device?

"Is the cone completely bolted in?" he asked Gabe, who stepped out of their way. "*¿Terminado?*"

"Yes," Gabe said, and rapped the handle of his wrench on the rim to show that it was solidly attached.

"Easy with that," Steve muttered, and gently set his side of the motor on the rim of the cone. "It sits inside," he said to Mason, "with the gearbox facing up."

It took them a minute to maneuver it into place, and once it was in, Mason saw that the cone had been specifically built to house the motor—it fit snugly, with no gaps around it. With Steve directing them, Gabe and Flaco bolted it in place, then installed a cover that left the gears protruding. More of the pipes were then attached to the gearbox and bolted to the ring around the bottom. Mason could see how the mechanism would work now: the cone was going to spin, while the cage-like structure of the pipes, attached to the ground, held everything in place.

"Looking good," Steve said, his excitement palpable. He had Flaco and Gabe bolt the two half-moon steel plates to the cone, near its tip, so they formed a disk-shaped platform a few inches above the ground, protected around the perimeter by the fixed ring of steel pipe. It looked like a crazy person's merry-go-round. Mason grinned as he took in the overall construction. Working as a psychic seemed bizarre sometimes, but it was mostly cerebral—this thing was physically, tangibly bizarre.

Finally the assembly was complete, and Steve had the guys resume digging the trench. He walked slowly around the device, carefully prodding and pulling on it, examining the bolts, running his hand along the pipes.

"Can you get the grease gun from the garage?" he asked Mason.

"Sure—what does it look like?"

"It's blue, and cylindrical. I think I left it on top of the arc welder."

He stifled the urge to ask "What's an arc welder?"

and walked into the garage. He found an oily-looking blue tube with a hand pump and a short black hose sticking out one end, sitting on top of a squat red box labeled MONTCLAIR ARC WELDER. He brought it out to the yard and passed it to Steve, who attached the hose to the gearbox and pumped the handle, presumably filling it with lubricant. He did the same at the bottom, where the cone was mounted. Finally he stepped away, tossing the gun to the ground. Despite the hot summer day, he rubbed his hands together, as if he were going to touch a living thing and didn't want to startle it with cold hands, and then gave the edge of the cone a solid sideways push, walking partway around the device to get it moving. When he let go it continued rotating, smooth and silent.

"Ha!" Steve cackled, clapping his hands. "That's what we call precision machining, baby."

"Is it working?" Mason asked.

"Not yet, but now we know it'll work the way it was designed." He went back into the garage and came back with electrical conduit, which he laid in the trench while Flaco and Gabe dug the last few feet. Mason fetched tools and parts when Steve asked him to, but mostly he just watched. An hour later, they'd hooked up the wires at the base of the device.

"The moment of truth," Steve said, mopping sweat from his brow. "I'm going to turn on the breaker—shout if anything weird happens." But he didn't move, and stood staring at the device. "On second thought, why don't you go flip the breaker,

Mason? It's the bottom one on the left side. I want to see it start up."

Mason strode to the garage and found the breaker on the electrical box. He snapped it on and waited. A moment later there was a loud whoop. Back in the yard he found Steve dancing around the device, which was rotating now, faster than a merry-go-round but still at a sedate pace.

"It's working," Steve shouted, fists pumping skyward. Gabe leaned on his shovel and laughed in amazement at Steve's glee.

Mason grinned too, watching him strut around. "Should we be able to feel anything different?"

"You tell me," Steve said, pausing his celebratory dance. "You're the psychic."

"OK," he said, and put his hands on his hips, watching the device. Counting in his head, he estimated it took three or four seconds to make a full revolution. He closed his eyes and spent a few minutes tuning in to the node below it, clearing his mind and focusing on direction-finding again. It seemed the same as before, no stronger or weaker. He could hear the motor in the device, a soft metallic hum, but there was no other mechanical noise. The gears and bearings were precision parts, Steve had said.

"I can't sense that anything has changed," Mason said.

"Not yet," Steve said, "but it will." He had calmed down, and directed the guys to fill in the trench. "Once we put the canopy over it, the work is done."

He looked at his watch. "I think that'll have to wait till tomorrow, though."

The two of them stood in silence, watching the device spin; the only sound besides the quiet hum of the motor was of Gabe and Flaco shoveling dirt. Steve was entranced, Mason saw. It really was an arresting sight, such a bizarre device, spinning and seemingly doing nothing. Gazing at it was hypnotic. It was all about circles, layers of them: the base, the disk, the cone. They symbolized perfection, circles did, as well as eternity. That couldn't have been Steve's intention—to an engineer, circles and disks were utilitarian, their shape intrinsic to a rotating machine. Still, it was beautiful, and eerie.

When Gabe and Flaco had finished filling in the trench, Steve had Mason go into the garage and snap off the breaker. The machine took a few minutes to slow to a stop, and once it did, they pulled a tarp over it and pegged the corners into the ground. Mason helped put the tools and leftover bits of wire in the garage, and Steve moved the truck inside the garage and closed the door.

"Money," he said, and strode toward the house. He reemerged a minute later with a fistful of cash and paid Gabe and Flaco, who thanked him and headed toward the street.

"Good-bye, *brujo*," Flaco said with a wry smile.

"Not a *brujo*," Mason called after him, pulling on his backpack.

"You kind of are," Steve said.

"I'm not going to cop to that without knowing the implications. I'm a psychic. I'm pretty sure it's completely different."

He laughed and counted out a stack of bills, handing them to Mason. "I wanted to wait until they'd gone before I paid you," he said. "You charge a lot more than they do. Hey, are you hungry?"

"Very," Mason said. "I missed lunch."

"I don't have anything here, but there's a diner two blocks away. Would that be OK for you?"

"I can make it work."

"Let's go out through the front," he said, surveying the yard one last time before leading Mason into the house. It looked like an ordinary backyard again, no longer a construction zone, and the tarp-covered structure wouldn't attract undue attention from anyone walking through the alley.

The house looked lived in, but it certainly wasn't homey. Mason waited in the kitchen while Steve went into the bathroom to clean himself up. Rather than cups or plates, the kitchen table was covered with fiddly little tools, machine parts, screws, and spools of wire. The living room was littered with unpacked moving boxes, the only concession to ordinary life a sofa and a TV.

Steve came back, looking fresher in a clean shirt, and he followed Mason out the front door. The diner at the end of the street was old-school, with a long counter and red leatherette seating that looked like it hadn't changed in decades. A young woman in a waitress's uniform greeted Steve by name. She nodded to an empty booth and they slid in.

"You're already a known entity in the neighborhood," Mason said.

"I've been eating here a lot. I'm not much of a cook."

They ordered beer, and Mason asked for plain oatmeal and French fries, the only vegan things he could find on the menu. Soon the beer was in front of them, and they clinked their glasses. It tasted perfect after a long day in the sun.

"I'm still not clear on what the machine is actually doing," Mason said. "To me it looks like it's just spinning in midair."

"Having that much metal right above the node point is significant. The metaphysical properties of metal are that it's unyielding, and forceful, but also transformative—as a psychic you can pick up information from metal objects, right, and you can't do that with something made of earth, like pottery, or with wood."

"Right." He was impressed that Steve knew this. Psychometry was one of the more esoteric tools in his repertoire.

"Adding the rotation allows it to overcome the force of the earth and resonate with the lines. Metal comes from the earth, so spinning it reverses the relationship, and the strengths of the metal can flow down into the node." He had that look in his eye again, the spark of a man obsessed. "Imagine things from the perspective of the cone. If you're the cone, you wouldn't have the sensation that you're moving. Everything else, everything around you would be spinning—the node, the yard, the city, the entire planet. Imagine that kind of power."

The waitress set down their food, and Mason dug into the oatmeal. Steve took a bite of his sandwich, but Mason could tell he wasn't thinking about it. He was buzzing, surely from what they'd achieved today, and perhaps from having a confidant to talk about the project. He took a long drink of beer and continued.

"The rate of spin is significant too. The motor is calibrated to rotate at a specific multiple of the fundamental frequency of the ley lines, so they resonate, and the machine can transfer their energy."

"The technical part of it is over my head, but I get the gist of it. I have to wonder, though, what's in it for you? Surely there's more to it than amplifying good vibes."

"The other function of the machine," he said quietly, "is to fix the node in place."

"And that's a good thing?"

His eyes grew wide. "Of course it is. Think about the implications—for the first time in human history, the lines will stop their eternal wandering. It'll benefit all of us by stabilizing and focusing their power."

"I can see how that would be a remarkable achievement," Mason said, pushing his oatmeal bowl away and switching to the fries.

"Unparalleled," Steve said, his eyes shining. "And

I'll be the person who achieved it."

Mason nodded, and Steve took a bite of his sandwich and stared into the distance, lost in thought. Maybe he wasn't the Fool after all, Mason thought, but the Death card. Its meaning had little to do with actual death, he'd found in his reading—rather, it implied transformation, and Steve definitely wanted to transform the world.

"Do you know what happened in Detroit?" Steve asked finally.

"Today?"

"No, I mean generally, over the last thirty years."

"The economic decline? Yeah, they made robots to build the cars and fired all the people."

Steve nodded. "But there's more to it. There used to be a first-order ley line running right through that town, but in 1960 it started to drift away. By 1990 it had moved hundreds of miles. That's why the city declined."

"OK," Mason said, sipping his beer. His own simpler explanation seemed more plausible.

"If the machine works the way it's supposed to, Los Angeles will be protected from that. The first-order lines won't drift away, and the town won't lose its vibrancy."

"How did you learn about all this?"

"There are theoretical books about the lines, and I got worried when I read about Detroit. I thought it through, and applied the expertise of my own field to the problem. The machine is mostly my own design."

He ate the last of his sandwich and wiped his mouth on his napkin.

"You must be happy to have it finished."

"Oh, it's far from complete," he said, his eyebrows rising. "I have to get a backup generator so it'll keep spinning when the power goes out. That's the easy part. The real work is going to be amping it up with group-3 metals. I'm going to mount them all around the rim of the disk. It's going to take a while—they're expensive, and I'll have to have the pieces precision-cut."

"What are group-3 metals?"

"Group 3 is a column in the periodic table, elements that share certain properties—most significantly, they all have hexagonal crystals. They're really good at concentrating psychic vibrations. Right now the machine has the impact of something like a car battery, but with those metal slugs attached, it will be like a whole power plant. It'll focus cosmic energy and pump it into the node."

"What will that do?"

"More energy, more good vibes." He smiled. "In my perfect daydream world, it'll spark a golden age of creativity and prosperity, all emanating from my backyard."

"How will you know if it's working?"

"You're the detective," he said, leaning back in his seat. "Once I've installed the new metal parts, I'll get you to come back and figure out how things are progressing."

The waitress appeared at their table. "Another round, boys?"

"Nah," Steve said.

She grinned at Mason and set the check folder between them.

"Damn it," Steve said, groping around in his pants pocket. "I left the house without any dough. I'll run back—give me two minutes."

"Let me buy your dinner," Mason said. "You just paid me for a day's work—I'm feeling flush."

Bleary-eyed, Steve assented with a grateful nod. Mason dug his wad of cash out of his pants and tucked some bills into the folder. He pulled on his backpack as they rose to leave. Halfway to the door, the waitress called after them, "Sir, could I speak to you for a moment?"

She had the check folder in her hand, and gestured to the other end of the counter.

"Was your card declined?" Steve asked.

"I paid cash," Mason said. "But you should go— you look exhausted. I'll handle it."

"Thanks, man," Steve said, and squeezed Mason's arm. "And thanks for coming over. I couldn't have done it without you."

"Of course," Mason said, smiling. It felt good to be appreciated.

Mason walked to the far end of the restaurant, where the young woman was standing in front of a stretch of the counter devoid of customers. A bright yellow pencil was tucked into her tight afro above one ear. The absurdity of it made him smile.

"Was my cash counterfeit or something?" he asked as he approached.

"No," she said quietly, her eyes darting toward the kitchen. "I overheard your friend mention that you're a detective. I need a detective."

"I don't love that word," he said. "It makes it sound like I'm peeping in people's bedroom windows. I call myself an investigator."

She frowned. "You think that *doesn't* make you sound like a window peeper?" Her enunciation had shifted from unremarkable broadcast English to a South LA street dialect. Whether she had intended that to be humorous or not, it made him laugh.

"I guess you're right," he said. "It's basically the same thing." He fished in his pocket and found a dog-eared business card, handing it to her.

"Nice to meet you, Mason," she said, resuming the broadcast dialect. "I'm Julia. So are you Steve's boyfriend?"

"No—I'm doing some work for him."

She nodded. "Steve doesn't seem gay."

He grinned. "But I do?"

"Well, you haven't looked at my breasts even once, and that's kind of the point of leaving a few buttons open. The tips are better when you show a little cleavage."

Involuntarily Mason looked at her chest and quickly looked away. "Stately," he stammered, feeling his face turn red. "Well-deserving of larger tips."

Smirking at his fluster, she looked back to the card and tapped it with her finger. "A psychic investigator. Hmm."

"I do regular old investigating too," he said. He was finished working with Steve, and he couldn't pass up the prospect of a new job. "What is it that you need to find out?"

"First I should ask what it'll cost me. I'll have more scratch after you find what I'm looking for. Is there any chance I could pay you then?"

"No," Mason said flatly.

"Well, then, what do you charge?" she said, putting her hands on her hips.

"That depends on what the job is." He wasn't going to drop his usual day rate on her and frighten her off. She was hustling for tips in a diner, which meant she probably had limited resources. If the job was straightforward, he could scale back his rates.

"Right." She bit her bottom lip and looked away, considering. "It's kind of a proprietary thing. I don't want to give away the idea unless I'm sure you'll be working for me."

"And I can't tell you whether I can help you unless I know what the job is."

Her eyes narrowed. "Can't you pick it up psychically?"

Mason laughed. "I wish it worked that way."

"Let me think about it," she said. "I'll figure out what I can afford to spend, and then I'll pitch you the case."

"That's fine," Mason said, and smiled politely. "You have my number."

"I will call," she said, meeting his eye. "I just need to get organized."

She probably wouldn't, he thought, as he walked back toward Steve's place. She seemed too uncertain. But he liked her energy and her quick wit.

He let himself in Steve's front gate and found his bicycle beside the house where he'd left it. Even though it was still daylight out, he could see a faint, fluttering blue light reflecting on the wall of the house next door. It had to be coming from Steve's backyard. Was it the machine malfunctioning? He waited and listened, and the light flickered again, but there was no noise. Rather than walk back there uninvited, he pushed his bike out to the street and climbed on, then rode around to the alley to look over the fence. The machine was still safely under its tarp, unmoving. The blue light flashed again, out of sight behind the garage, and now he could hear the faint *zap* of electric current. A hazy plume of smoke curled above the garage roof. Steve was back there welding, he realized. The guy was driven.

He cycled back to the metro, and waiting on the platform, felt his phone buzz in his pocket. It was a text from Ned:

Home for dinner?

He wrote back,

Be there in thirty.

It was hard to believe that Steve's machine was actually going to accomplish anything, especially something as grandiose as ushering in a golden age. His explanation of its workings had been a jumble of ideas, a box of crayons spilled on the floor. It would be difficult even to sort out how much of it was evidence-based, as Ned called it. But he knew the supernode was real—he'd seen it, felt it. If he knew that part of it was legit, how could he discount what Steve was doing?

When he got in, Ned was wearing his cooking apron, stained with the evidence of many meals, and Peggy was setting everything out on the dining table—corn on the cob, tomato and tofu caprese, and arugula with shredded carrots.

"I'm glad you didn't eat yet," Ned said, pausing to kiss him hello.

"I had a late lunch," he said, setting his backpack down by the door. It had been less than an hour ago, but he wasn't going to let that keep him from enjoying the spread.

When they sat down to eat, Ned talked about his lunch with his family, and then asked Peggy how her day off had been.

"I went hiking with Psychic Matt," she said.

"How's it going with him?" Mason asked.

"So far, so good. This was our third outing."

"No red flags?" Ned asked with a grin, passing her the arugula.

"No red flags … yet." She smiled.

"Do you talk about psychic stuff?" Mason asked.

"He said he wasn't allowed to talk about psychic power with nonpsychics."

"No one ever told me that," Mason said, frowning.

Ned chuckled. "It sounds like he was joking."

"I think it just means he doesn't want to talk about it," Peggy said, setting down her corn. "He gets my music, though, and that's huge. He actually got us invited to a hootenanny."

"What the hell is a hootenanny?" Ned asked.

"People get together and play folk music."

"What's exciting about that?" Ned said. "You could do that yourself, with your friends."

"The people who put them on are beatniks from back in the day, so they're seniors now. They've been doing it for decades, so they're highly skilled. Playing in someone's living room without any equipment is so intense, so authentic."

"It sounds perfect for you," Mason said, scooping tomatoes onto his plate.

"It is. In my world, a beatnik hootenanny is the gold standard."

"Are you going to perform?" Ned asked.

"I'll have to. There are no spectators—if you go, you perform."

"In the Peggy Pregnant outfit?" Mason asked. Her stage persona, Peggy Pregnant, had played small venues around town for years wearing a massive faux baby bump and flower-child garb, strumming an acoustic guitar and singing folky tunes. It was a dramatic visual.

"I'll have to do it without the belly. I'm a little nervous about that—I'll feel naked without it."

"It might feel more authentic that way," Ned said.

"Maybe," she said. "Anyway, I'm totally impressed that Matt is getting us in. It'll be a blast."

"I'm impressed that he even knew such a thing existed," Ned said. "I've never heard of it."

"It's a big city," Mason said.

Ned looked up at Mason. "So how was your day with Uncle Steve?"

Mason told them about the device, and helping assemble it. "He was still working when I left. I'm exhausted, and I didn't exert half the effort he did today."

"It sounds insane," Peggy said. "He's just going to leave it running in the backyard?"

"He's going to put a canopy over it, so it won't be visible to snoopy neighbors and people going by. It doesn't make any noise or anything."

"That doesn't make it any less insane," she said.

"I have trouble buying it myself. I know the node is there, because I've seen it. I just don't know whether the device will actually do anything."

"Human nature is so weird," Ned said. "He's basically a scientist, but he's trying to harness psychic energy. Where's the disconnect?"

"Maybe he thinks psychic energy *is* scientific," Mason said.

Ned scoffed. "It's more like those people who say Jesus had a pet dinosaur. They twist something that's scientific up with something that comes down to irrational belief."

"To me it sounds like he's an amalgam of contradictions," Peggy said. "It's not his fault. We all are."

When Mason got into bed later, he relaxed comfortably into the mattress, his body appreciating the calm after an active day. He folded his hands under his head, staring up at the ceiling. It was amazing that he'd managed to float right through that.

"You seem spaced out," Ned said, climbing in beside him.

"Just tired," he said, turning toward him. "I wanted to ask you about a Latino thing—one of the workers today called me a *brujo*. What does that imply, exactly?"

"What was the context?" Ned said, moving closer and wrapping an arm across Mason's belly.

"He saw me do my psychic thing, locating the node in Steve's backyard. He didn't look upset, just surprised."

"I don't think it means he's going to run to a priest to exorcise you or anything. A *brujo* has a legitimate job in a traditional community."

"So a *brujo* is like a shaman?"

"Those are two different jobs. My understanding is that you'd go to a shaman if you had a health problem or an existential crisis, but you'd go to a *brujo* if you wanted something material, like a boyfriend or a promotion at work."

"I'm not really that kind of psychic," Mason said.

"I don't think you can legitimately call yourself a *brujo* either. It takes a lot of work to learn those procedures. It's like you can't just call yourself an accountant, or a paramedic. You have to do the work to earn it."

Mason murmured assent and kissed him good night. Ned picked up his novel, and Mason rolled over to switch off the lamp on his side. He knew sleep would come quickly.

Feeling himself sliding into the hypnagogic state, he reminded himself to wake up inside the dream world. Soon he was following a long, thin line, stretching away toward nothingness. He drifted along it, looking for the end. It was straight, like the ley lines, but different somehow—it wasn't in the earth, he realized, and there was nothing tangible around, like the ground or the sky. There was just the thread, flowing toward nothingness, going on forever. He lost track of it eventually, not becoming aware enough to manipulate it, and not remembering more.

SIX

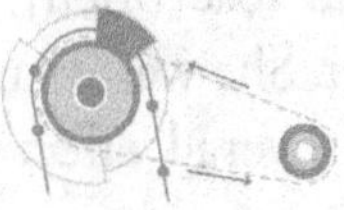

When he became a full-time psychic, Mason's first client had been Miss Cassie, a shrink. Even though he'd been new at it, he'd managed to help her out, locating her estranged daughter, and in return she'd cajoled him into becoming her client. He didn't always feel like going to talk to her, and he didn't always understand what she was trying to do, but he knew there was value in their sessions, and it helped him stay grounded. Besides, it had become nearly automatic; he budgeted for it, and just had to click "Accept appointment" when he got an email from her calendar. He had a session with her today.

Her office was in a renovated art deco tower

downtown, and if nothing else he loved being transported to that glammy place for a fifty-minute hour every week or so. He locked up his bicycle at the metro station in his neighborhood and rode underground, emerging across the street from her office. When he took the elevator up, he found the sliding sign on her office set to COME IN, so he slid it across to PLEASE KNOCK and pushed open the door. Miss Cassie was sitting in her usual chair, beside the tall windows that looked out at the towers of the financial district.

"Mason," she said, a warm smile on her face. "Come on in." She rose briefly, and he sat on the sofa across from her. She was wearing a dark suit with a bright scarf, the overall effect deemphasizing her ample weight.

"How're things?" she began, reaching for her tablet and sliding out the stylus.

They talked about some of their ongoing discussion points: his stress level, how things were going with Ned.

"How's work?" she asked.

"I just wound up a case for a guy who hired me to look for an earth energy structure. He was quite happy with my results."

"Is he hunting for oil?" she asked, scribbling on her tablet.

"He built a device to interact with cosmic energy," he said, and explained what ley lines were, and what Steve hoped to accomplish.

"He's investing his time and money doing this?"

"A lot. He bought a house based on what I told him."

She stopped writing and looked at him for a minute.

What had he said? She was never at a loss for words, and she always made a point to keep the conversation moving. Too bad his psychic skills didn't extend to being able to read her mind.

"Tell me more about this client."

"I can't tell you his name. I'm bound by client confidentiality."

She suppressed a grin. "In general terms, then."

"He works as an engineer for some Korean outfit at the port. So he has an education and a decent job."

She nodded. "Is he partnered?"

"No, he lives alone. His house looks like his garage—tools and machine parts everywhere."

"Does he spend all his time working on this earth energy machine?"

"Well, I'm sure he has to go to work sometimes."

"Is he secretive about it?"

"Totally. He doesn't want anyone to see the device. I don't blame him: it would elicit a lot of questions. I probably shouldn't even be talking about it."

She sighed and set down her tablet. "It sounds like this fellow is delusional."

"He's a regular person," he said sharply. "He's not garbage—he just has some nontraditional ideas."

"I'd never say he was garbage, Mason. 'Delusional' is a word we use in clinical diagnosis."

Mason could feel his cheeks burning. "You don't know the guy. How can you diagnose him?"

"You're misconstruing my words." She paused to rub her eyes, and looked tired. "Do you remember where we first met?"

"I came to your church in Leimert Park."

"One of the things you hear in black churches is, 'God doesn't make any junk.'"

"Which means—what?" he asked.

"That everyone has value by dint of their humanity. In religious terms, it means no one is beyond redemption. But more broadly, it means that no one is worthless—no one is garbage."

"That's good."

"It's not a judgment—I've never met him. My concern is that, from what you told me, it sounds like he might be mentally ill."

"He's fine," Mason said. "He's completely functional." If she could be dismissive of his psychic skills, he could be dismissive of her instant diagnosis.

"I understand that's what you see." She looked at him thoughtfully. "The question for you is, are you making things worse for him by feeding the delusion? Leading him on, taking his money?"

"My god, woman," Mason exploded. "After all we've been through together." He took a couple of deep breaths, and tried to lower his voice. "I am not a fraud."

"I know that," she said gently.

"He would've bought the house anyway," he said,

shouting again. "He would've hired someone else to find the right spot."

"But he hired *you*. He paid you for your exclusive access to the psychic world."

"Not true," he said, throwing his hands in the air. "You were talking about your church—anyone can have a personal connection to god without a priest as intermediary. No exclusive access."

"At least since the Reformation," she said.

"It's the same approach—anyone can develop psychic skills."

"Anyone?" she said dubiously. "You don't need any special gifts or talents?"

He thought for a minute. "Maybe it's like playing the guitar," he said, calmer now. "Some people have a predisposition to do it really well, and some people have to practice a lot more, but theoretically anyone can learn it."

She nodded, her gaze back on her tablet, scribbling notes.

"I'm getting more skilled as time goes by," Mason said intently. "I get stronger signals, and I get the answers more quickly." He looked away. Why did he feel the need to defend himself to her?

"So it's all positive?" she asked.

"The only downside is that things are getting weirder. I can't even articulate how weird—the people I meet, the things that happen. If I tried to explain it, I'm afraid you'd just see more mental illness."

"Why not try me?" She looked up and smiled.

How could she be so mean and stay so calm?

"Reality is starting to look like a kaleidoscope," he said, "only I'm completely immersed in it. To function in the world, I have to break focus and remember what most people consider to be real."

She watched him for a moment, deep concern in her eyes. "In a way, you're telling me that you're losing touch with reality. That's a serious matter."

"I'm fine," he said emphatically.

"But you don't always remember what's real."

"That's not what I said."

"I'm going to give you my evening number," she said. "I want you to call me if you get into trouble."

"I don't see that happening," he said, but he pulled out his phone anyway and typed in the number as she recited it.

"Just keep it in the back of your mind if anything difficult comes up. If you get angry, for example, and can't contain it, or if you feel sad to the point that you can't function. Any encounters with the police." She smiled gently. "If you get stuck in your kaleidoscope and can't figure out what's real."

"None of those things have been happening to me," he said, frowning.

"Well, if they do, call." She looked up at the wall clock and set her tablet down. "It was so nice to see you."

"Right," Mason said, realizing their time was up. He said good-bye and walked out to the elevator lobby, pausing to slide her door sign to COME IN.

He still felt flushed as he rode down to the street and made his way back to the metro. Maybe he was going to have to stop seeing her, or at least give her less detail about the strangeness of the work. She had reacted so strongly—he hadn't anticipated that. He didn't want to wind up in a psych ward.

On the train he found a seat and watched the tunnel walls flashing past. It was a grim thought, but the farther he got from the mainstream, the less he was going to be able to trust mainstream people.

Ned was home when he got back, and came out of the office.

"You're sweating," he said, reaching up and running his fingers through Mason's hair.

"Not surprising," Mason said irritably. "It's hot out."

"OK," Ned said, pulling his hand away. "How was Miss Cassie?"

"She kind of freaked me out," Mason said.

"What did she say?"

"Lots of things," he said, gesturing vaguely.

"Coffee?" Ned asked, heading into the kitchen.

"Yeah." Mason sat at the counter and watched Ned fire up the espresso machine. "The gist of it is that I'm going to have to be more careful about how much I tell her about my work."

"You can't lie to your therapist," Ned said, furrowing his brow. "It defeats the purpose."

"I'm worried she'll have me locked up."

"She wouldn't do that, sweets. There's no reason to."

Mason sighed. "Let's hope not," he said, and reached for the mug Ned handed him.

Before Ned could respond, Mason's phone rang. He pulled it out of his pants and went over to the sofa with his coffee. He didn't recognize the name on the screen, but answered anyway, "Braithwaite."

"I told you I'd call," said a familiar voice.

It took him a second to place her. "Julia. The caller ID showed a completely different name."

"Yeah, my phone's in my sister-in-law's name. Anyway, I think I can explain my project for you now. You can tell me what it'll cost, and then I can say, 'I can't afford it.'"

Mason laughed. "Don't get ahead of yourself. What's the project?"

"Have you worked a missing person case before?"

"I have," he said. "Has it been reported to the cops?"

"No, because she's been missing since 1998."

"Wow. Is it a relative?"

"No—I never met her," she said. "Listen, Mason, can we meet in person? That way I could explain things clearly and show you what I've got."

"Sure."

"The only thing is, it has to be after six."

"I guess I could do that," he said, looking toward the kitchen, concerned that it might interfere with dinner.

"I'll give you a street address," she said, and rattled it off.

Mason rose quickly and went into the office to get a pen. He pulled a yellow notepad out of his desk and flipped to a clean page.

"That's in Hollywood, right?" he said, scribbling it down.

"Yes—it's a bank. I'll meet you around back in the parking lot, a little after six."

"I'll be there. You've got me intrigued."

"That's me—a riddle wrapped in a gluten-free enigma, with a sprinkle of mystery flakes."

"That's pretty mysterious," he said, chuckling at her humor.

"See you soon," she said, and hung up.

On his phone he found the name and number she had called from so that he could copy it onto his pad. At the top of the page he wrote "Julia," and under that, "missing person."

"You got another gig?" Ned asked, standing in the doorway to the office.

"It might be," he said. "I'll find out this evening."

He stuffed the notepad into his backpack, then scooped up his laptop and went out onto the balcony. It was warm out here, but not unbearable.

He had found an online copy of the tarot book he'd borrowed from the library, with pictures of the cards and synopses of their meanings. He opened the book now and scanned it, looking for something that reminded him of Julia. It was entertaining to read, but after a while he set it aside. He didn't know her well enough to identify her with specific traits, but he had the notion she could be associated with the suit of wands, because she seemed creative and lively, like the wands were. He had turned up the Page of Wands when Anna had read for him, and the card, representing a free spirit, could easily be Julia.

Eventually it got too hot to sit outside, and he went in to put away his computer. Hollywood wasn't far, so he decided to bike rather than take transit to go meet Julia. He pulled on his backpack and said good-bye to Ned, who was still working.

"What time is dinner?" Mason asked him.

"Whenever you get back. Text me when you're headed home."

When he pulled up at the bank, it was just after six. It looked dark inside, but there were still quite a few cars in the parking lot, which was shared with the neighboring businesses, he realized, and some of them were still open.

Julia came out of the building as he was locking his bike to the rack near the ATMs.

"You must live nearby, if you're on two wheels," she said. She was dressed in a plain blouse and dark blue slacks, the same color scheme as the bank's signage, and toting a bulky black handbag. Her vest bore a little name tag, embossed with the bank's logo and JULIA.

"Not far," he said, and grinned. "So you're a banker as well as a waitress."

"Glamorous outfit, isn't it?" she said, touching her name tag. She looked back at the entrance and said, "So, we're going into the bank, but not quite yet."

A uniformed security guard came out and locked the door behind him with a jangly key ring. He nodded to Julia, then strolled toward the ATMs.

"It looks kind of closed," Mason said.

"It is," she said quietly. "I work here as a teller, part-time, so I have access to the building. But let's wait in my car for a second." She glanced furtively at the retreating guard and then led Mason toward the back of the lot. Her vehicle was a beater, a nondescript decade-old subcompact, dented and dusty, parked by a hedge about as far from the bank as possible. He climbed in the passenger side when she opened it for him. At least it was clean inside. He fumbled to find the control to adjust the seat, moving it back so his knees weren't on the dashboard.

Julia slid down in the driver's seat, peering through the steering wheel. They had a clear view of the bank building from here, and she watched it intently. The guard had disappeared from view.

"Bear with me," she said, as if reading his mind, not breaking her gaze. "I'll explain everything in a minute."

"OK," he said. He looked at the bank, trying to see what had captivated her attention, but there was nothing happening, no one in sight. He looked her over. If she worked in there, why was she skulking out here? For a fleeting moment he wondered if she was planning to rob the place—but that was absurd.

"Your hair is different," Mason said.

"Oh, yeah, I put some product in it today," she said, touching it absentmindedly. "I can let it go wild for waiting tables, but bankers are more conservative."

"No cleavage today either."

She laughed, still focused on the building. "They want me to look upscale, but they don't pay upscale. Do you have any idea how much it costs to get black hair done at a salon?" she asked, glancing at him.

"I can't imagine."

"A lot, to get it done right."

They sat in silence for a few minutes, and Mason shifted uncomfortably in the cramped seat.

"So, how about that baseball team?" she said finally, still watching the bank.

"'That baseball team'?" he asked, incredulous. "Julia, I don't know anything about baseball, and you don't even know the name of the local team. What are we doing here?"

She sighed. "I didn't want to seem underhanded."

"Sorry, but that's exactly how you seem," he said emphatically. "We're hiding in your car."

"There," she said suddenly, her voice dropping to a whisper, even though no one could have overheard them. She slid lower.

Mason watched as a conservatively dressed woman with a big shoulder bag came out of the bank, locked the door, and walked to her car.

"Who's that?" he asked.

"The manager." They watched her back out of her parking space and drive out of the lot onto the boulevard. "She had to leave before I can go back in."

Julia opened her door. "Let's go," she said, the tension gone from her voice.

Mason climbed out and stretched his back. "So the place is empty now?" he asked.

"There's the security guard, but he hangs around the lobby and the ATMs. He won't bother us." She set off confidently across the parking lot, her handbag pushed up on her shoulder.

"Are we supposed to be doing this?" Mason asked nervously, catching up to her. It felt like they were about to burglarize the place.

"It's fine," she said.

"There are security cameras all over the building. I can see three of them from here."

"Nobody ever watches the video unless there's an incident," she said. "It just sits on a server."

Sneaking in after hours could be defined as an incident, he thought. But she worked here, and she seemed to know what she was doing. More importantly, he had no inkling at all of foreboding, which happened to him sometimes around sketchy people.

Rather than walking to the main entrance, she went the other way, out of sight of the ATMs but still in view of at least one security camera. Mason glanced up at the lens, aware that there was no hiding from it. On the side of the building was a fire door, and in seconds Julia had produced her keys, unlocked it, and heaved it open.

"Come on," she said quietly, waving him inside. She pulled the door closed after he stepped in.

Inside was another door, probably leading into the bank, and a flight of stairs leading down into darkness. At least the little space was free of cameras. A lighted keypad was beeping at them insistently. Julia punched in a code, and it fell silent.

"It's a low-security alarm because it's just for the basement," she explained. "There would be a lot more noise if we tried to get into the actual bank."

She flipped a light switch beside the alarm panel, illuminating the stairway, and began trotting down, Mason close behind her. It was a sizable space, he saw, as big as the building above. What did this place have to do with Julia's missing person?

"This is the cooling system," she said, gesturing to a squat and bulky machine bristling with air ducts and pipes painted in bright colors. They walked past a row of uniform storage cabinets along the wall.

Toward the back of the basement was a chain-link fence separating a dim space that looked a lot messier than the bare and well-swept floor around the machinery. Through the fence Mason could see boxes and crates stacked among indeterminate masses draped in dusty canvas. The gate into the cage-like space was also chain-link and bore the grime of decades, but the padlock on it looked new. Julia used her keys again to unlock it, then pulled it off, glancing toward the stairs and then locking it again to the fence. She pulled open the gate, but rather than walking in, she stopped and turned to Mason.

"Julia, what is this place?" he asked.

"This building used to be a radio studio back in the day. They broadcast all over the country. When a radio studio dies, what do you suppose they do with the remains?"

"The equipment? I don't know. If it were me, I'd sell the good stuff, and send the rest to a landfill."

"Or you could just move it into the basement and forget about it," she said, grinning and walking into the cage.

He hesitated for a moment but then followed her in. It was crowded, but there were paths on the floor to walk among the piles. He stopped and looked around at the mess, taking it in. Boxes, junk, and dust—nothing that would merit a second glance. It was quiet down here, the only sound the distant hum of the cooling equipment.

"That's what all this is?" he asked. "The leftovers of a radio station?"

"More than a station," she said, setting her handbag on a stack of boxes. She clicked on an overhead light by pulling its chain, instantly making the space less ominous. "A national studio. It was shut down in the early sixties, and the bank has been here for twenty years or so. But none of the tenants over the years bothered to clean out this stuff."

"How do you know all this?"

"From digging through it." She threw back the corner of a canvas sheet and pulled out a heavy disk-shaped object, darkly tarnished and with wires hanging from it.

"A microphone?" Mason guessed.

"Exactly. And look at this," she said, setting it down and pulling the canvas off another pile to reveal what looked like a piece of antique furniture, dark wood inset with heavy switches and analog meters behind age-crazed glass. "This was a sound board, circa 1950."

"It's very cool," he said, running his fingertips over the polished wood. "How did you find this?"

"They sent me downstairs to put things into the storage cabinets, and I got to poking around. I had to, uh"—she sought the right word—"update the lock."

"You broke in, and put on your own lock."

"No," she said, frowning at him. "I just swapped out the padlock. I'm not going to steal any of this stuff. It belongs to the bank now, not that they care that it's here. My interest is in the historical value."

"I wonder if any of it is worth anything," Mason said, looking around.

"Maybe, but that's not my concern. I'm happy that it's been forgotten. If it sits here a while longer, I can finish exploring it."

"When do you do that?" he asked.

She smiled. "After six."

"It's cool stuff, but Julia—what has it got to do with your missing person?"

Wordlessly, she walked over to a stack of cardboard boxes and opened the top one, pulling out something wrapped in newspaper, then whipped off the paper with a flourish. It was another microphone, similar to the one she'd shown him but smaller, this one standing on a wooden base. She set it carefully on top of a crate so that Mason could examine it.

"It's not actually a mike, right? It's an aluminum statue of one," he said, looking it over.

"Pewter," she corrected him. "It's a Radio Voice Award. Those went defunct when TV eclipsed radio, but back then, it was a big deal to win one. It's nicknamed a 'Yappie.'"

"Subtle," Mason said, raising his eyebrows.

"Read the inscription," she said, nodding at the object.

Affixed to the wooden base was an engraved gold plate. "Vanessa Barton, the Immortal Warbler of the Sierra Nevada, 1953," he read. "It doesn't say what she won it for."

"It wasn't subdivided into a million categories like they do today," she said. "'Best left-handed female vocalist in a cereal commercial.' The Yappies only gave out one award each year."

"You know a lot about the radio era," he said, looking at her again.

"After I found this room, I started reading up on

the studio that was here, and the industry. I practically lived in the library for a while."

Mason said, "I spend lots of time in the library too."

"The smell, the texture of old paper. The way a book's spine creaks when you're the first person to open it in fifty years."

He nodded, grinning at the thought. "I know."

"This woman, Vanessa, led such an interesting life," she continued, her tone growing animated, her eyes lighting up. "Her singing voice wasn't actually that amazing, but she did comedy routines and monologues, vaudeville-type stuff, and all of that was brilliant. I did so much research on her that I decided to write a biography. There isn't one."

"How cool," Mason said. "Were you interested in her before you found this stuff?"

"I'd never heard of her, and I didn't know anything about the radio era. It was serendipity to stumble on this."

Suddenly it clicked. "This is your missing person," he said. "You want to find Vanessa, the Immortal Warbler, so you can interview her for your book."

"I guess you really are psychic," she said, raising her eyebrows.

"If she won this award in 1953, she must be at least"—he did the calculation in his head—"in her eighties, right? Unless she won this when she was an ovum."

"Therein lies the mystery," she said. "Officially,

she died in 1998. But I know she's not really dead."

"How do you know that?" he asked, raising his eyebrows.

"There's evidence." She draped her hand protectively on the award. "All the newspaper reports of Vanessa's death at the time said that she was buried cradling her Yappie in her arms, because it was her fondest achievement."

"Clearly they were wrong," he said. "It's right here."

"You and I know that, but no one else would—except her," Julia said intently.

Mason didn't respond, waiting for her to continue.

She took a deep breath. "I was reading all these posts on an online forum—it's not specifically about her, but about the radio era in general. Someone asked why the Immortal Warbler's career had ended so abruptly, why her show had been canceled mid-season. Another user said that she'd had a falling-out with her producers. And then, someone else posted more, with so much detail—stuff I'd never read anywhere else. I tried to contact the poster, but the account had been deactivated by the time I found this stuff. Anyway, this person said she had an argument with the producers one morning, and walked out of the studio, never to return. 'She left with nothing, not even taking her Yappie.' That studio," she said, her eyes growing wide, "was in this very building."

"OK," Mason said, thinking it through. "Maybe

this was a duplicate Yappie given to the studio."

"They didn't do that," she said. "I checked. There's only one."

"Well, her producers would have known she left the award behind. Maybe one of them was your forum poster."

Julia shook her head. "If they'd noticed, or placed any value on the Yappie, they would have taken it, and it'd be sitting on someone's tchotchke shelf right now. Plus, I looked into everyone who worked on the show, and they're mostly all dead. It's so long ago, half their kids are dead too."

"Maybe Vanessa's kids knew the true story?" Mason said. "Or a good friend."

"She never had any kids," she said impatiently, and folded her arms. "I'm sure this seems kind of tenuous, but I know it's her, Mason. I can feel it."

He nodded. "I'm the last person who's going to discredit intuition. But why would she have faked her own death?"

Her face broke into a broad smile. "Let's find her and ask her."

He picked up the Yappie, turning it over in his hands, feeling the heft of it, considering the story. "Why did they call her the Immortal Warbler of the Sierra Nevada?"

"There were lots of singers with names like that back then. Edith Piaf was called the Sparrow, and there was a jazz vocalist called the Allegheny Meadowlark. Vanessa got her start at a little radio station in Bakersfield, and her producers thought 'Sierra Nevada' sounded more glamorous than 'the Immortal Warbler of Bakersfield.'"

"They were right."

"I'm going to use that story to open the book," she said, meeting his eye. "It's fascinating stuff, and it needs to be remembered—Vanessa needs to be remembered."

He nodded and set the award down. Julia picked it up and wrapped it in the newspaper again, placing it carefully back in its box.

"So, Mason," she said, turning back to him. "What is it going to cost me to have you find her?"

"It's hard to say," he hedged. The story was just so far-fetched. Vanessa probably really was dead, and there was no point in even humoring Julia.

"I don't make much money," Julia said, "and I've got student loan debt. But I've been putting money away. I call it my Immortal Warbler fund—to buy me some time off so that I can write the biography. I'd pay you out of that fund."

"Oh, Julia," he said, dismayed at the thought of draining her savings.

"What are your rates?" she demanded. "If you wanted a hundred bucks a day, I could pay you for two or three weeks. Or do you charge by the hour? How much time would you need to find her?"

He wasn't going to pocket Julia's cash only to find that Vanessa was dead after all. He couldn't do that to her. Miss Cassie had said it this morning: he would just be making things worse by feeding someone's delusion.

"I can't do it," he said.

She frowned. "Because you're not capable of doing it, or because you don't want to?"

"I don't want to take your money," he said.

"I'm the only one who gets to decide what I do with my money," she snapped.

"Fair enough."

More gently, she said, "Will you at least consider it? Take a look at what I've written so far, and think about it." She went to her handbag and fished out a sheaf of paper, handing it to him. It was stapled in one corner, maybe thirty pages thick, and bore the title "The Immortal Warbler of the Sierra Nevada" on the top page.

"This isn't the only copy, I hope?" he asked.

"Of course not—I'm writing about the 1950s, not living in them. That's just the start of the book, the bare bones."

"I'll read it," he promised, pulling off his backpack and sliding the manuscript inside.

"Just don't steal my idea," she said, and more emphatically, "and don't tell anyone about this stash."

"I won't."

He followed her out of the cage, waiting as she doused the light and snapped on the padlock. She swatted the dust off her dark trousers.

"Do you ever worry about getting locked inside?" he asked. "It feels claustrophobic."

"Oh, god, no. I have a pair of bolt cutters stashed in there—those things will cut through a wire fence like it was overcooked spaghetti."

They walked up the stairs, and she switched off the lights and reset the alarm.

"Play it cool when we walk out," she said. "Especially if the security guard is nearby. Act like we're supposed to be here, like we do it every day. If he says anything, I'll do the talking."

She pushed open the door, and they stepped out into the warm air. Mason glanced around nervously, but no one was in sight. It was still bright out, although the shadows were lengthening. Before she went to her car, Julia turned to him and held his gaze.

"Think about it," she said. "I'd really appreciate your help, and I can afford it."

"I will," he said, and watched her walk away. He sent Ned a quick text, "Home in twenty," then went to the other side of the building and unlocked his bicycle. He nodded to the security guard as he rode away.

When he got home he sat down to eat with Peggy and Ned, who'd made cold soba noodles with a dipping sauce as well as a tray of sushi rolls cut into neat bite-size pieces.

"Thanks for waiting for me," Mason said, happily moving rolls onto his plate.

"It's nice to eat later when it's hot out," Ned said.

"Tell me what the different rolls are," Peggy said.

"That's cucumber, and these are avocado, and the brown one is *kampyo,* a kind of pickled gourd," Ned said, pointing them out. "It's hard to find, so when I saw it today I knew I wanted to make them."

Mason changed the subject. "So, question: how should I set my rates for a person with limited resources? Do I use a sliding scale, or what?"

"Hell, no," Ned said. "You're not a charity."

"How limited?" Peggy asked. "And who is it?"

"It's the woman I met with today. She's working two jobs, her phone is on some relative's account, and her car is so decrepit I thought it would collapse when I sat in it." It was an exaggeration, but it illustrated Julia's means.

"What does she want you to do?" Ned asked, between mouthfuls of noodles.

"Find someone who faked her own death," he said.

"That doesn't sound like an essential service that a low-income person can't live without," Ned said. "Is it someone who owes her money?"

"It's someone she wants to write a book about."

"Then no discount," Ned said flatly. "Things are tough all over. You have to be able to earn a living."

"I'm doing that regardless," he said. "She's willing to pay my usual rates, but she couldn't do that for very long, and I don't know if I can take it from her. It's her savings—I'd feel like a vampire."

"It's kind of condescending to decide what she can and can't afford," Peggy said. "It's not your business."

"That's what she said, but I know her financial situation, and I'm not going to feel right ignoring it."

"Well, if you do use a sliding scale," Peggy said, dipping a roll in her little tray of tamari, "you can't get resentful about it. You have to do the work whole-heartedly, just like you would for someone paying your full rate."

After they'd eaten, Mason cleaned up, and Peggy retired.

"Want to watch *America's Filthiest People?*" Ned asked. "I saw the preview—this woman lives in her car in her own driveway because her house is completely hoarded out."

"That does sound like fun," Mason said.

"Educational," Ned corrected. "It's on the Learning Network."

"I think I'm going to read up on my case. But you'll have to recap the episode for me."

He pulled Julia's writing out of his backpack and settled onto the sofa. It was only about thirty pages, but as he got into it, he could see that she'd done a lot of work. The writing was good too—logical, concise, artfully illustrating Vanessa's personality:

> In February of that year Vanessa met Robert Norris, the respected Anglo-Indian author and biographer of the last Viceroy, in New York at a gala held to raise relief funds for those displaced by the war. Observers said the Immortal Warbler easily held her own with the literary titan, lucidly defending a political position that Norris had taken exception to. Illustrating his point, Norris said, "You must agree, Miss Barton, in

your culture it is said that a man cannot live on bread alone." Without missing a beat, Vanessa countered, "You are correct, sir—but in my personal culture, I'd need a big swipe of peanut butter on that bread, and maybe some half-sour pickles on the side. If he's single, you can send in that man you speak of too." With that, the Immortal Warbler deftly defused the contentious debate and shifted the conversation in a lighter direction, all without offending the great sage.

It must have been time-consuming to do all the research, and it was heavily footnoted, citing dozens of books, articles, and interviews that she'd conducted herself with industry people. Clearly Julia was serious about documenting the life of the Immortal Warbler.

He went into the office to get his laptop and brought it back to the sofa. The tarot book wouldn't help him decide how to handle the case, but he wanted to read more about the cards in the suit of wands. Rather than the Page, Julia seemed like the Ace of Wands, he realized as he read. The card corresponded well to her personality—she was creative, inspired to write Vanessa's biography. Even the card's imagery, a disembodied hand thrusting a wand into the world, paralleled her quest to create something from nothing: the life story of an obscure, forgotten character presented to the twenty-first century.

He closed the book and did a Web search for "bank teller" and "salary," confirming that Julia really did have limited income. The banks hired part-timers for those jobs so that they could dodge paying for health insurance, and a quarter of bottom-tier employees at banks were even eligible for food and rent welfare subsidies. He searched for the sister-in-law who was paying Julia's cell bill by using the name that had come up on caller ID, and turned up a street address in a hardscrabble neighborhood in Long Beach. Her relatives weren't wealthy either.

He folded his computer closed and stretched out on the sofa. He couldn't ask her to spend her savings, he was sure of that now. But it was a compelling story, Vanessa faking her own death. It seemed far-fetched, but he had to remind himself not to trust the skeptical reaction, and instead to look past it for more insight. That's what he would do: he'd look into the Immortal Warbler without asking for money. If there was anything to it, maybe then he'd figure out a way to get paid. He'd keep it to himself—he certainly wasn't going to tell Ned he was working for nothing. Hopefully it wouldn't take too long to get some answers.

Getting into bed later, Ned straddled him and playfully mussed his hair.

"Hey, norimaki man," Mason said. "Did *America's Filthiest People* get you turned on?"

"Nope—just you," he said, and leaned in for a passionate kiss.

After they'd had sex, as he was drifting into sleep, Mason told himself to wake up inside his dreams. *Get some insight,* he told himself.

He was walking in a park, with trees and rolling lawns, tall buildings in a row in the distance. Central Park, he realized, coming to some awareness. New

York. There was Anna, standing under a tree, unmistakable in her burgundy caftan, looking up into the branches.

"Hey, Anna," he said, happy to see a familiar face. "What are you doing here?"

She smiled knowingly, and looked back into the tree. "She's right here."

"Who's that?" he asked, looking up and seeing no one.

"The Star," she said. He looked again, but there was nothing but leaves and branches and birds. They were singing, he realized after a moment. It wasn't especially pretty, but it was birdsong.

He lost the thread and eventually woke up, clicking on his bedside lamp and pulling his notepad out of the drawer to write down the details before they evaporated. "The Star is in New York," he wrote. "In a tree. And Anna." He thought for a moment, and then added, "Ask her if she was really there."

He assumed he'd quickly get to sleep again, as he usually did, but he lay there, looking at the window, the faint glow of daylight creeping into the room. It must be very early morning. Why was he so awake?

At that moment a dark shape entered the room, stepping out of nothingness. His heart started to race. There was no detail, no face, just the outline of a person, a man. It wasn't just the darkness of the room obscuring his features, there was really nothing to see—he was a silhouette made of pure darkness. It hadn't come in, it had just materialized, moving purposefully—Mason knew that this was a supernatural being. The figure sat on the easy chair opposite the foot of the bed, his dark shape obliterating the chair's vague gray bulk. The shadow man put his head in his hands, as if deep in thought. *Who is this?* Mason wondered, anxiety growing, and the figure seemed to react to the question, dropping his hands, sitting up straighter. Mason's heart leapt when he sensed the figure turn toward him.

"So, chump," the shadow man said. "Are you making things better, or are you making things worse?"

Mason tried to scream, but nothing came out. Then he was awake, the light of dawn creeping in the windows. Had that actually happened?

His heart was pounding—the fear had been real. He sat up on one elbow and looked at the easy chair, unoccupied. Eventually he decided it had been a dream. He looked over at Ned, who was still sleeping soundly. Miss Cassie had really undermined his confidence today, if he was having threatening visitations that threw her words at him. He looked at his pad on the night table with his earlier notes. He couldn't bring himself to write down that he'd seen the shadow man. That would be embracing self-doubt, admitting it was valid. But he knew he wouldn't soon forget about it either, and it took a long time to get back to sleep.

SEVEN

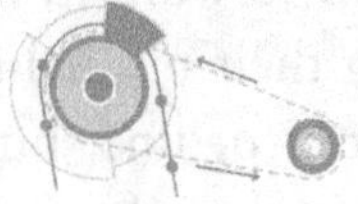

When he woke up later, the full light of day had washed the darkness out of the bedroom, and looking at the easy chair now he could hardly believe the shadow man had felt so real. Thinking about it still made him uneasy, though. It could have been an entity dropping into his room, or into his subconscious, which was a distressing thought. The simplest explanation was that it came from his own mind, that Miss Cassie had struck a nerve.

He was not going to crawl into that hole, he decided. The only way to overcome self-doubt was to climb over it by achieving something else, to get to work. He got out of bed and made coffee, ate some fruit, and went into the office. Ned was on the phone, so he took his computer out onto the balcony and pulled up his tarot book. He read about the Star—its connection to immortality, how it might have been an ancient Egyptian reference to Sirius. He got sidetracked reading about Sirius, visible mostly on winter evenings.

He set his computer on the table and stretched in his chair, looking out over the neighborhood. Maybe the Anna in his dream hadn't been talking about the Star from the tarot. He considered calling her to ask if she'd actually been in his dream, but thinking about how to word it, he knew he'd sound nutty. Considering their mutual profession, it probably wouldn't be out of line, but maybe there was another way to parse the information.

On a hunch, he grabbed his computer again and pulled up the map of the ley lines he'd made for Steve. He'd drawn two of them, intersecting in what was now Steve's backyard. The brightest one ran generally east-west, but when he zoomed out, it definitely trended northeast. He extended the line on the map, dragging it across the continent, perfectly straight. He'd dreamed about New York, but the line didn't run anywhere near that city; instead, it crossed the Great Lakes and into the North Atlantic at Labrador. It had been worth a try.

But he was missing something, an idea, lurking just beyond his perception. He closed his eyes for a second and willed it to well up in his mind. Looking at the map again, the line was straight. Ley lines were straight, but only when you looked at them from above. They followed the curvature of the earth, so they were really circles, rings—like the circles of Steve's spinning machine. He opened the map's settings, and in a few keystrokes had adjusted the line to follow the earth's natural shape. He zoomed in on Steve's neighborhood. The line was still anchored right under his lawn, and under the end of the 605. Following it east, it ran farther south now, through Pennsylvania, crossing into the Atlantic south of Nantucket. With growing excitement he zoomed in closer, and found the line now passed through New York City. It missed Central Park, cutting a mile or two north of it through a neighborhood the map labeled Sugar Hill.

He smiled to himself, amazed at the elegance of it. It had to be meaningful, dreaming about that little island and then finding Steve's ley line ran right under it. He had wanted insight into Julia's research, and even though it was counterintuitive that the Immortal Warbler was linked to Steve's quest, from another angle it wasn't weird at all. Unseen connections ran through the world, and what seemed like a coincidence maybe wasn't. Julia knew Steve, had introduced herself after seeing Mason with him. And if this much synchronistic information was bubbling up, maybe there was a reason—perhaps Vanessa really was alive.

He dialed Julia's number and got her voice mail. "It's Mason," he said. "I read your intro, and it's pretty impressive. I'm going to check into Vanessa and see if I can get some insight as to whether she's alive. I'm still not convinced that you're right about that, but I think it warrants a hard look. As for money—let me figure out if I can learn anything, and then we'll talk about the cost. For now, though, I'll do some preliminary digging, and I'll let you know."

He hadn't rejected the possibility of getting paid, but at least he'd postponed worrying about it for both of them. He folded his computer closed and took it into the office to put it on his desk.

"Lunch?" he asked Ned.

Ned looked up from his computer and shook his head. "I have a meeting out, so you're on your own. There's leftover soup in the fridge."

Ned left soon after, and Mason found the soup, heated it up, and ate at the counter. His phone buzzed in his pocket, and he wiped his mouth before pulling it out to answer. It was Matt.

"We've been summoned to Pretty Nail Blowout for a planning meeting," he said. "Can you drop by there in an hour or so?"

It was Hanh's salon, not far away. Matt had warned him this was coming.

"Does it have to be today? I've got a lot going on. I just got a break in a case."

"Don't be a flake, man. You know this is important."

Mason sighed. "I'm sure it is. Yes, I'll swing by."

"Good answer," Matt said.

"I just find that woman so intimidating."

"Who doesn't? She's a time-traveling badass. If you want warm and fuzzy, get a cat."

Mason chuckled. "I'll see you there."

An hour later he'd changed and set off on his bike, riding on side streets toward the salon, a nondescript storefront in a strip mall on Sunset Boulevard. He locked his bike to a tree on the sidewalk and pulled open the door under the sign for Pretty Nail Blowout. The woman at the front desk smiled in recognition.

"The red man," she said. "Miss Hanh is expecting you."

"My name is Mason," he said sharply.

"Of course," she said, nodding deferentially. "Miss Hanh is in the back."

A couple of customers were having their nails done, and one of the technicians smiled at him as he walked through, then said something to her colleague, evoking a titter. He didn't speak Vietnamese, but he was certain the amusement stemmed from his red hair. It was irritating. Surely he wasn't the only redhead they'd ever seen.

Matt was already there as he stepped into the back room, sitting with Hanh at the table that dominated the small space. It was essentially a storage room, with racks of towels and grooming products, a messy desk crammed into one corner.

"Hey, stretch," Matt greeted him.

"Am I late?" he asked, setting his backpack on a chair.

"Not at all," Hanh said, and gestured to the ancient coffeemaker incongruously perched on a shelf amid bottles of chemicals. "Help yourself."

She was always the same when he saw her, the wedge haircut and the serious tone. He poured himself a mug of acrid coffee from the grubby carafe and sat down with them. Matt was telling her an animated story about one of his students. He looked so comfortable chatting with this taciturn woman. It made him seem so much more proficient at the psychic thing than Mason was, and he didn't even do it full time. But he had run into the same pitfalls as Mason had, so maybe he just seemed better at it because he was more confident—which was probably part of why Peggy found him attractive.

"I have an errand to do late tonight," Hanh began, looking at them in turn, "and I need your help."

"That's why we're here," Matt said, and Mason nodded in agreement.

"There's a knucklehead who needs to be dealt with. His name is Ali, and he's figured out how to slip backward in time. He's hanging around the horse track, betting on races that he already knows the outcome of."

"That would get suspicious pretty quickly, wouldn't it?" Matt said.

"That's why it has to be handled. I'd like you two to come with me."

"What exactly would it entail?" Mason asked. "I'm not really qualified to be an enforcer."

"You won't be," she said. "I'm the heavy."

It sounded absurd coming from her, a little slip of a thing, but he knew she had nerve.

"I need you two for your energy. Like when we did the séance."

"Which race track?" Mason asked, furrowing his brow.

"The one that's been demolished," she said. "He's not here-now. He's operating about fifteen years ago."

"Is he from then?" Matt asked.

"I think so. I've only picked up traces of him moving backward and forward in a very limited time range."

Mason wanted to ask how that worked, but he held his tongue; he knew she wouldn't tell him, or would use some obtuse metaphor to explain.

Matt wasn't so reticent. "If it happened that long ago, why does it matter now?" he asked.

"The flow of time is just how our minds interpret reality," she said. "On a deeper level, everything is happening at the same time."

Mason thought about that for a minute, trying to absorb it.

"Our brains filter out the complexity," Matt said finally, looking glum. "That's kind of depressing."

"It allows you to function," she said. "It's actually an elegant way of navigating reality."

"So why is the past fixed but the future isn't?" Matt asked.

"We can only focus on a few things at once," she said. "If the past wasn't fixed, we couldn't focus on anything. It lets us deal with one thing at a time. Even our languages are linear. One word or phrase follows another."

"Not sign languages, though," Matt said. "They can transmit several ideas simultaneously."

Mason watched, fascinated, as they discussed whether that made sign languages truly nonlinear or not. Hanh gradually convinced Matt that they weren't. Mason had never seen Hanh so candid. Eventually she steered the conversation back to Ali and their errand.

"The stupid part of it is that he doesn't even need the money," she said. "He's the scion of a Middle Eastern royal family. He's doing it for his own amusement."

"So what exactly are we going to do when we find him? You'll be the authority figure, but what about us? I have so many questions," Mason said, feeling overwhelmed.

"How about this," Matt said to him, and then turned to Hanh. "Is it going to be dangerous?"

She considered that for a moment. "I'd say probably not."

"There you go," Matt said, looking back to Mason. "That's the only question that really matters. Let's just do it, and take it as it comes."

"OK. I'm in," he said, trying to channel Matt's certainty, then draining his mug. Hanh's answer wasn't unequivocal, but he trusted both of them enough to go along with it. It was flattering to be asked to help because of his psychic skills, and to sit in on Hanh's mind-bending understanding of reality. Hopefully he'd learn something in this, provided he managed to get through it in one piece.

"We'll meet here tonight at eleven," she said, rising from her chair. "Come around to the back door."

Mason pulled on his backpack and set his coffee mug beside the sink. He said his good-byes and was about to step through into the salon.

"Could you two go out the back way?" Hanh asked. "It's less disruptive for the customers."

"Sure," Matt said, and Mason followed him to the fire exit at the other end of the room.

"It's the red hair," Mason said, once the door had slammed shut behind them. "That's what's disruptive."

"You're too sensitive," Matt said. "I'm sure it's not about you."

"Every time I go in there, her staff freaks out, like some mooky Sasquatch just walked in."

"You don't look like a Sasquatch," Matt said.

They walked out of the dead-end alley back toward the boulevard. Mason stopped beside his bike and pulled out his keys. "Where did you park?" he asked.

"I'm on the train, man. At this time of day it would have taken three times as long to drive."

"I'll go with you, then. I'm going downtown."

Mason unlocked his bike and rolled it between

them as they walked. "You don't seem at all worried about this excursion tonight," he said.

"I'm sure it'll be straightforward, but who the fuck knows?" He eyed Mason's bicycle. "It's funny what scares people. You're willing to bike down Sunset fucking Boulevard at rush hour, but standing behind Hanh while she admonishes some degenerate blue blood has you worried."

"I guess it's the unknown part. I know what to expect in traffic."

They trotted down the stairs into the metro station, Mason carrying his bike, and waited for the train.

"Do you think that's all we're going to do—talk to the guy?" Mason asked.

"It sounded like that to me. What did she call it, 'an errand'? That's simple enough. What's more concerning is whether we're going to be doing this a lot. Do you get the feeling we've been deputized?"

"I hadn't thought of that," Mason admitted.

"It's the first time she's asked me to help out. How about you?"

"The only other time was that séance for you during the whole Billy Blood thing."

"You know, I have a theory about her," he said. "Have you heard of the garuda?"

"Indonesian, right? A mythological bird?"

"It's not just Indonesia. There are tales about them throughout Asia, in Buddhist and Hindu traditions. They're not really birds—they're bird-headed supernatural beings with specific powers. But that changes in every version, and there are dozens of versions. They can take human form when they need to deal with our fucked-up loser species. And they're responsible for policing paranormal activity."

"You think Hanh is a garuda?"

He shrugged. "I don't know. It kind of fits."

"I'll have to read about them." Mason chuckled. "Does that make us assistant garudas?"

"I think we'd know that, if it was a formal position, don't you think?"

"Maybe we'll find out tonight," he said. "So how's it going with my roommate?"

"Great," Matt said, his tone brightening. "She's a lot of fun. We're going to a hootenanny."

"I heard."

They boarded the train and rode downtown, Mason disembarking at the library, Matt continuing toward his place in the Arts District. Climbing up out of the ground, Mason felt his phone buzz, and when he pulled it out he saw that Julia had left a voice mail.

"I am so glad you're taking this seriously," she said. "I'm ecstatic that you're going to work on it. Let me know when you need some dough."

He grinned to himself, feeling uplifted by her enthusiasm as he cycled toward the library.

He locked his bike to the rack outside and found a desk in the history department, where he pulled out Julia's manuscript. It took some time to assemble her original sources, but many of them were here, and eventually he had a pile of material to wade through. It was a lot of reading. He scanned through the parts that seemed less relevant, and discarded other volumes entirely. One book, about the radio era, dedicated a whole chapter to the Immortal Warbler, including a full-page portrait. It was clearly a manicured publicity shot, in black-and-white, but he got a sense of her from the image. The photographer had positioned her carefully to minimize the fact that her wide-set eyes were asymmetrical, one slightly higher than the other, but it was still detectable. That alone explained why she hadn't moved from radio to film, but her gaze was sincere, and there was a hint of humor in her expression. Seeing her made him curious to hear her voice.

"Vanessa," he said under his breath. *Are you still alive?* The portrait had no answers, but he pulled out his phone and photographed it for his file.

The sources on microfilm he left for last. The librarian pulled the spools, then Mason got set up on a reading machine. Soon he was scrolling through copies of decades-old newspapers. On the third spool, one of the articles—from the late 1940s, when Vanessa was first becoming known—talked briefly about her roots in an old moneyed Northeastern family. He sent the page to the printer and rewound the film. Pulling his laptop out of his backpack, he balanced it next to the microfilm reader, then looked for information about her family, the Bartons.

A lot had been written about them when the

family had been most prominent, during the first Gilded Age, several generations before Vanessa. Libraries had been built, colleges endowed. Fluff pieces gossiped about the family's society parties, or hinted darkly about their undue political influence. There had been a summer estate in Newport, and a townhouse in New York. One of the articles said it was "a lovely home in Harlem" with "high windows overlooking Colonial Park," and named the architect commissioned to design it. That was enough information that he could probably locate it, if it still existed, but was that a worthwhile detail? He sent the item to the printer anyway.

A cursory Web search for the architect quickly turned up "the Barton townhouse" among his credited works—that had to be it. It still stood, and architecture aficionados had posted the street address and an array of exterior photos. He went to a mapping website and typed in the address. The house was at the north end of Manhattan, in the Sugar Hill neighborhood—he had just looked at that on the map when he'd extended Steve's ley line across the country. With growing excitement he pulled up the map he'd made with the line and zoomed in on the Barton townhouse.

"Whoa," he said, stunned. Scrolling in, he found that the line went directly under the house—not just close, not grazing a corner, but perfectly bisecting the structure. He sat back and stared at the screen.

For a while now he had fully embraced the

existence of such strange, unanticipated connections, but seeing it laid out so blatantly, displayed with the impartial precision of technology, was startling. There was so much going on beyond what he could perceive. He closed his eyes for a few seconds and could almost feel it, the massive workings of the universe, like a machine whirling all around, just outside perception. In practical terms, the meaning was clear: there was something important here, something to be found—and he had to keep digging.

The townhouse. After some hunting he was able to pull up property records for it, and soon he was in a database with title info dating back to the time of the Civil War. A string of Bartons had owned the house until the 1970s, when it was put into a trust named Barton Sugar Hill, still the title holder today. Despite conducting an exhaustive search, he couldn't find out who actually lived in the townhouse. Possibly it was unoccupied, but more likely it was just well-protected information. He saved a copy of the document, then folded his computer closed.

It was well after business hours on the East Coast, but tomorrow he'd call the trustee that was listed in the property record, a pompous-sounding three-name law firm. If the trust had the family's name on it, there were probably still Bartons around who benefited from it, maybe even living in the house. If Vanessa really was alive, it could even be her. Maybe that's what Anna had meant, standing under that tree—Vanessa, the radio star, was in New York.

At the counter he returned the spools of microfilm and paid for his printouts, sliding them into his backpack and heading up to street level. He took a couple of the books about the radio era with him, checking them out before heading outside, where he found an empty bench in the library's little garden, shaded by old trees and the office towers of the financial district looming above them.

He could let it go until tomorrow, when he could talk to the trustee, but he felt too much momentum now, and there were other ways to get information. Pulling his phone out of his pocket, he found the number for Danny Santos, a journalist he'd recently worked with. He was a childhood friend of Gilbert and Ned who wrote for a weekly paper called *Va-Voom*.

He picked up with a curt "Santos."

After they'd exchanged pleasantries, Mason asked, "How hard is it to find out who lives at a specific address?"

"Not too difficult. Why?"

"What if the address is in New York?"

"Still not too difficult. Are you asking for my help?"

"Well, I figured you kind of owe me a favor, seeing as I helped you with that article, exposing a corrupt corporation and all that."

"Your input was useful," Santos said guardedly.

"Without my input there wouldn't have been a story," Mason said. "Didn't you win some journalism award for it?"

"Not yet, but I did get nominated." He sighed. "What exactly do you need?"

"The name of whoever is living in a house that came up in one of my cases. It's really straightforward."

"I should be able to find it using the paper's resources," he said. "And lucky for you, I'm in the office today. Do you want to swing by?"

"*Va-Voom* is on Twenty-First, right? I'm just a few blocks away. I'll be there in a couple of minutes." He could feel his heart pound at the tantalizing possibility of getting an answer. He knew he was asking a lot from Santos, but Mason used to work with journalists, and he knew they tended to thrive under pressure.

Stuffing his phone back in his pants and pulling on his backpack, he went to the bike rack and unlocked his wheels, riding the short distance down to South Park and the two-story brick building with VA-VOOM emblazoned on the facade. A hundred years ago it had probably been a warehouse, but today it was repurposed as chic, creative office space. Locking his bike near the front door, he walked inside and asked the guy on the reception desk for Danny Santos. He gave Mason the once-over and waved him in, not bothering to check with Santos, buzzing him through the security door.

It was probably a good thing that he came off as innocuous, Mason reminded himself as he trotted up the stairs, even though it might be nice once in a while to cast the kind of shadow that struck fear, or at least suspicion.

The office was quiet, which meant they weren't approaching a publishing deadline. Mason found Santos in a cubicle, hunched over a keyboard. He had dark hair, like Ned, and was dressed like someone who didn't spend a lot of time in the office, in jeans and a plaid shirt. Mason did a double-take at the oversize monitor in the next cube, displaying a full-screen image of a half-naked model with garish makeup and a louche expression on her face. A young woman was carefully positioning black asterisks over the bodacious exposed breasts.

"Holy erotica, Batman," Mason said.

Santos turned around. "That was quick," he said, peering at Mason over his reading glasses, and to his colleague, "Lin, this is Mason."

She pulled off her headphones and said hello.

"Are you doing a story on porn?" he asked her.

"I do ad layout. They're working girls," she said, and turned back to her screen.

"Ads for prostitutes?" Mason asked.

"Escorts," Santos said. "Have you looked at the back third of *Va-Voom* lately? If it weren't for escorts and strip clubs, we'd all be unemployed."

"I just read it for the award-winning articles," Mason said.

"Grab a chair," Santos said with a wry grin, gesturing to one in an empty cubicle.

Mason pulled it over and sat with him. Santos asked him for the address of the Barton townhouse, and Mason watched as he searched a database that he'd never seen. It had a lot of detail about the property, much more than he'd had access to at the public library.

"Everything's in the name of this trust," Santos said finally. "The title, taxes, everything."

"That's as far as I got too."

"They may be trying to obscure the name of the resident, but there are other places to look."

He spent a few minutes digging, with Mason admiring his deft keyboard work. The guy was fast and efficient at parsing the data that came up.

"Here," Santos said, pausing at a list of house numbers and names. "This was compiled by the city's rent control board."

"I doubt that the townhouse is a rental," Mason said.

"Doesn't matter. The board collects the names of everyone living in every unit regardless."

"That seems intrusive."

"It is, but don't kid yourself—the big tech companies are doing the same thing, they're just not as sloppy as local government about exposing it."

He scrolled down the screen to the entry for the townhouse. It had two names: Nissoué Louloune and Meg Martel.

"You did it," Mason said, and clapped him on the back. "Nice work."

"Do you want me to print it?"

"This is easier," Mason said, and pulled out his phone to photograph the screen. "So how difficult would it be to get a photograph of these two, now that we have names? Maybe from a driver's license or a passport?"

"Difficult," Santos said, leaning back in his chair. "And illegal."

"It's not like I'm going to publish it. Besides, you're a journalist—when did the law ever stand in your way?"

He chuckled. "I found the names for you, which means I've officially repaid your favor. I'm not going to break the law for you."

"I broke the law to help you bring down Billy Blood," Mason said. "The wiretaps—surely they were illegal. That packet of evidence was pretty huge compared to the amount of work it took to find these names. Not that I'm ungrateful," he said, raising his eyebrows.

Santos watched him for a minute, considering. "That was a mighty big story," he said finally.

"I saw your byline in the national media. Journalists were interviewing *you* about the story."

"True," he said. "Tell me this: why do you need to see photos of these people?"

"The job I'm on is a missing person. If I can see a photo of her, I'll know whether I've got the right person or if I'm completely wrong."

Santos nodded. "OK. I know a guy. It involves a gratuity of two hundred bucks."

"I can swing that. Who gets the money?"

"I'll handle that. And you can't tell anyone I was involved."

"Of course," Mason said, and pulled his wad of cash out of his front pocket. He peeled off two hundreds and folded them lengthwise, handing them to Santos.

Santos glanced over his shoulder at Lin, but she was oblivious, headphones on, engrossed in her busty ad design. "I feel like a prostitute," he said quietly.

"Escort," Mason corrected him.

Santos frowned and nodded toward his computer screen. "You need to see both of them?"

"If it's possible," he said.

Santos pulled out his cell phone and tapped and swiped at it, then held it up to his ear.

"It's me," he said. "Can I get a couple of photos? One is a woman named Meg Martel, probably Megan or maybe Margaret." He spelled out Nissoué's name and rattled off the address of the townhouse. "Same address for both … No, just the photos … Thanks, man, you're a saint." He ended the call and set his phone on the desk.

"Is your source at the DMV?" Mason asked. "Or some police agency?"

"Do you seriously think I'm going to tell you that?" Santos said, incredulous. "Have some respect."

Mason held up his palms. "Just curious."

"I'll have it for you in the next day or two. Until then," he said glancing pointedly at his computer screen, "I've got work to do."

"Right," Mason said, and stood up. "Thanks for your help, man."

"No worries. And hey—we're even now."

"For a few minutes of keyboard work and one little phone call? Maybe … but if the photos don't show up, I want my Benjamins back."

Santos laughed. "It'll show. Now get out of my office."

Mason trotted down the stairs, nodded to the receptionist, and stepped out into the fading daylight.

Once he was home he had dinner with Ned, vegan mac and cheese with broccoli rabe on the side, and told him a little about his research into Vanessa and about seeing Santos, omitting the bizarre overlap with Steve's ley lines.

"I have a thing with Hanh tonight too," he said, finishing his greens. "We're meeting at eleven."

"Another séance?" Ned asked. "Why so late?"

"I think certain times of day work better for psychic stuff." It wasn't a total lie, just an omission. He had no idea why Hanh wanted to meet at night, and had no desire to explain what they were really going to do, then to have to wade through an interrogation only to face Ned's inevitable, insurmountable wall of disbelief.

After dinner, he considered taking a nap before his outing, but he was too wired in anticipation. Instead he stretched out on the sofa with his laptop and looked up the garuda. There were indeed dozens of versions, as Matt had said, but the common threads were the bird imagery and the supernatural powers. In some tales they were warriors responsible for policing "the underworld," which he knew was often shorthand for paranormal phenomena in general. It was an interesting idea, and made as much sense as any other theories about Hanh.

Next he hunted for any trace of Meg Martel, but she flew under the radar, not participating in social media, not showing up even in broad Web searches. He found a couple of Nissoués, but they were both in Haiti, with no connection to New York. Giving up, he searched for recordings of the Immortal Warbler. He found a site with episodes of *The Vanessa Barton Show,* and put in his earbuds to listen for a few minutes. It was a variety program, with music and comedy, interspersed with ads for toothpaste and laundry soap. She had a passable singing voice, but listening to her talk was more enjoyable. The format was dated and the jokes were corny, but her rich voice and careful intonation were captivating. She didn't sound like she was from New York, or Bakersfield, for that matter; she spoke with standard broadcast enunciation.

He put his computer aside and spent some time flipping through the books he'd borrowed about the radio era. It seemed the vaudeville style of comedic dialogue had endured a lot longer on the radio than in film, and the Immortal Warbler was one of many who performed in the genre. One of the books had photos of people working in the studio spaces of the building that later became Julia's bank. The equipment looked exactly like what she had showed him in the basement.

Eventually he set the books aside and got dressed. He tried to find a shirt that would fit in where they were going, fifteen years ago, but as he looked through his side of the closet, he was dismayed at how nondescript his clothes were. It didn't really matter what shirt he chose, which pair of ill-fitting trousers—they all had the same timeless vibe.

After he said good-bye to Ned, he mounted his steed and headed down the hill. He hated riding at night, after a recent incident when a corrupt bureaucrat he was investigating tried to run him over with a truck, so he waited for the bus on Sunset. Happily there was a space on the bike rack of the first bus to pull up, and soon he was unloading it again in front of Hanh's strip mall. He locked his bike to a sign near the bus stop and walked around back, into the dark alley. An ancient two-door hatchback was pulled up at the salon's back door. He banged on the heavy door, hoping Hanh could hear him from inside. Matt walked into the alley behind him and called out a greeting. Mason whirled around, startled, just as Hanh appeared.

"You're both here," she said. "Good." She slammed the door behind her and went to the driver's side of the little car. "One of you will have to sit in the back."

"I will," Matt said. "Mason's taller than me."

"I'd probably do better back there, because I can stretch out," Mason said, and flipped the passenger's seat forward, stooping down and awkwardly climbing in. It wasn't too uncomfortable once he'd found space for his knees. Matt gingerly flipped the seat back, careful not to hit Mason with it, and got in.

"This is quite a car," Matt said to Hanh. "It must be thirty years old."

"Twenty-four," she said, and shifted into gear, the tiny engine straining as she pulled out of the alley and onto the boulevard.

"If you want to swing by a scrap yard, I have fifty bucks—maybe we could trade up."

"This car can do things you can't even imagine," she said.

"I can imagine it disintegrating on the freeway when we hit sixty," Matt said.

"Quit trash-talking my car," she said, irritated. "What you see isn't all there is. You should know that."

Mason looked around the vehicle with interest. The windows were remarkably clean and free of cracks for such an old car. Even Ned's windshields—which got cleaned often, whether they needed it or not—weren't as perfectly transparent. It was almost as if they had been recently replaced, or were made of something other than glass.

"It's interesting that you say that," Mason said, leaning forward. He thought about the shadow man, appearing in his room unbidden from the unseen recesses of reality. "I can feel it, you know? There's so much evidence of it."

"You mean psychic stuff?" Matt asked.

"I mean all the things we can't see. Don't you get the sense that we're only picking up a tiny part of reality? Even though we see deeper than most people, there's still so much more."

"You want to look behind the veil," Matt said.

"There you go," he said. "That's a great analogy. Mostly I just get glimpses now and then."

"You can definitely see more," Hanh said, "but it changes things."

"You mean it'll change me?"

"You, your priorities, your values—everything."

"It sounds like that's how you do what you do, Hanh," Matt said. "You see more than we do."

She didn't reply, accelerating down the ramp onto the freeway, then merging across several lanes of traffic. They couldn't have been doing more than about seventy-five, but in the low-slung subcompact it felt like they were flying.

"So how do we look behind the veil?" Mason asked, talking loudly over the road noise. Matt looked at her expectantly.

"You have to tune in," she said.

"OK ... how?" Mason asked.

"Yeah, I think we need specific techniques," Matt said.

"Try using your inner senses," she said. "You can defocus your regular senses for a minute by ignoring them. Then you should be able to tune in to another layer of perception."

"Interesting," Matt said, and launched into a story about how he'd been meditating to sharpen his senses.

Mason tuned him out; he wanted to try the technique. Hanh had never before given him anything practical, which made her words all the more valuable, potentially a precious pearl of wisdom. He closed his eyes and spent a few minutes figuring out how to ignore his senses. It wasn't easy, but after a while he had the feeling that he was doing it, floating in stillness, disconnected from the conversation, the rattling of the car, the headlights flashing by. *Tune in to the inner senses,* she'd said. Gradually he got a new sense of the things around him—feeling them, almost like a thought but more substantial, more permanent.

In front of him were luminous balls of energy, scintillating blobs: one neat and tight, the other woolly and unfocused—Hanh and Matt. Below them a red line stretched out ahead, like the ley lines but not straight, winding off into the distance. It was the freeway, or symbolic of it. Below it was a matrix of lines and shapes, continuing farther down, layer after layer. The rubber-band ball. He noticed what must have been the car, a perfect ring encircling them all, rotating like Steve's device, solid and steady and flawless, nothing like the jalopy he perceived with his physical senses. There was more to the vehicle, he thought, more than he could perceive, either within the car or connected to it, filaments streaming away in all directions.

A dull sound reverberated through to his consciousness, and at the same time a ripple, a vibration ran through the messy blob where Matt was sitting. Matt was laughing, Mason realized, and forced himself back to his regular senses. He opened his eyes.

He felt shaken, lightheaded. If that was the essence of things, or even just a deeper look, maybe he wasn't ready for that level of perception.

They were on the transition road to another freeway, the familiar ramp arching at least a hundred feet off the ground, and because traffic was light Hanh took it at top speed. He'd driven this route many times in Ned's cars, but it had never seemed so precarious, and he fleetingly regretted leaving his altered state for this tangible world. The city streets below loomed at an exaggerated angle because of the steep bank of the curving ramp, and looking out the car's pristine windows right now was terrifying.

"There's a vegan soul food joint somewhere around here," Matt said, apparently unconcerned with Hanh's driving.

"Yeah," Mason said, looking away from the window. "Near the racetrack."

"The racetrack is gone, though, isn't it?"

"It's a giant construction zone right now, but the Forum is still there."

"That's where we'll park," Hanh said, keeping her

eyes on the road, and thankfully both hands firmly on the steering wheel.

"So how did this Ali guy figure out how to slip backward?" Mason asked.

"The same way we did, I suppose," Hanh said, glancing at him in the rearview mirror. "Most people know how to behave themselves at the fringes of reality. You knew, although I had to remind you. It just takes one idiot to seriously screw things up."

"Cheating on a horse race causes that much trouble?" Matt asked.

"When you're breaking causality, yes," Hanh said emphatically. "It's like throwing a hand grenade. Ripples and repercussions radiate in all directions."

She exited the freeway and drove on surface streets toward the Forum, a massive indoor stadium surrounded by a desert of parking. The building was dark and abandoned at this hour, the parking booths unstaffed, but Hanh pulled up to one of the entrances anyway. She pulled a key card from her visor and swiped it on the card reader, and improbably, the arm flipped up for her.

"Sweet," Mason said.

She drove diagonally across the empty lot and stopped far from the stadium, near the construction fence and the dark void beyond it.

"This is where the track used to be," she explained, and switched off the engine. She turned sideways to look at them both. Even in the dim light he could see the glint in her eye. She looked energized, ready for battle. Mason could easily imagine her as the warrior garuda.

"So what's the plan?" Matt asked.

"First we're going to find Ali. I'll try to get him to listen to reason. If he won't, or if he tries to get away, that's where you two come in."

Mason could feel his heartbeat accelerating. This was starting to sound risky. "To do what?" he asked.

"Channel all the energy you can into me. If I need it, I'll say 'now,' and you'll have to be quick." She looked at them in turn. "This is important. Don't think about it, don't hesitate, and don't hold back."

Mason thought he knew what she meant, even though he'd never really done it before. If they focused on her, they could support her, and she could tap their power for a brief time, like at a séance. He still craved clearer instructions, though, and considered asking her how to do it effectively, but he already knew what her answer would be: "Just make it happen."

She and Matt got out of the car, and Matt held the seat forward so Mason could climb out. He arched his back and stretched his arms, relieved to be out of the confined space. The acres of barren asphalt stretched away to the dark stadium. It felt odd to be in a place designed for so much activity when it was empty.

"Join hands, boys," she said, and they stood in a circle. "Clear your minds and follow along."

Matt grunted and screwed his eyes shut.

"It's easier if you close your eyes," Hanh said to Mason.

He obeyed, and before he'd even started to clear his mind, everything shifted. He felt the heat of the sun on his back, and when he opened his eyes the night was gone, along with the construction fence, and there were people milling around everywhere. They were still at the edge of the parking lot, but it was jammed with new-looking old cars. Judging from their vintage, she'd hit the right point in time. Weirdly, Hanh's hatchback was among them, right where she'd parked it, just as battered and still old, even here. In the distance rose an awning-covered grandstand: the racetrack. He'd never been, being averse to horses being used that way, but its shape was unmistakable.

Matt laughed and let go of their hands. "Fuck me," he said.

A guy in baseball cap looked at them quizzically as he walked past, and Mason wondered if he'd seen them appear out of nowhere. But it wasn't that. He turned to his companion and said, "I think they're praying." The three of them holding hands in the parking lot had caught his eye, but no one else paid them any attention.

"Why didn't anyone notice us?" Mason asked. "We just materialized in the middle of a crowded place."

"Stay close," Hanh said, ignoring his question and walking through the gates, heading across the plaza toward the grandstand, weaving through the food vendors.

"How are you going to find him?" Matt asked.

"I know he's here. I can smell him," she said.

Mason wondered if she meant that literally or metaphorically. He imagined a raptor seeking its prey, floating on thermals high above and diving for it once detected. They followed her toward the grandstand, taking in the crowd. Angelenos here didn't look that different than they did where they'd come from. Some of the clothes had evolved, although lots of people were wearing jeans like Matt's. Overall, the clothes seemed tighter, and there was more hair.

"Hey," Matt said to Mason under his breath. "I dare you to go over to that pay phone, call your own number, and say, 'Dude, buy a fuckload of Google stock.'"

"That would go over well," Mason said. "I'd find myself on the receiving end of a mission just like this."

Hanh stopped and waved them closer. "That's Ali. By the wall," she said, nodding toward a swarthy man leaning against a pillar outside the grandstand, not far from the entrance where people were coming and going. Hanh had said he was Arab royalty, but he was dressed like a Westerner, in chinos, tacky alligator-skin shoes, a lime-green polo shirt. One foot propped on the wall behind him, he was looking at a booklet and writing in it with a stubby pencil.

"Ready?" Hanh asked, eyes locked on her quarry. Not waiting for an answer, she took a deep breath and strode over to him.

Matt followed close behind her. He seemed

focused but calm; Mason could feel his own heart pounding, but walked right beside him, squaring his shoulders.

"You've been a naughty boy, Ali," she said, putting her hands on her hips.

He looked up, his eyes flicking over her, and glanced at Matt and Mason before replying. "Who the fuck are you?"

"I've come to ask you to stop cheating. You know what I'm talking about—stepping out of sequence."

He frowned. "How do you know about that?"

"You're causing trouble for people who are more skilled at it than you. You have to stop."

Ali snorted, his disdain palpable. "I'll do whatever I want."

"Your actions are causing damage," she said firmly.

He stood up, face contorted in a sneer. "What are you going to do about it, woman?"

"Ask you politely to stop," she said. "If you won't, we'll escalate."

He stepped toward them, towering over Hanh, menacing with his frame. Hanh didn't flinch. Ali glanced at Mason, and then Matt, looking them up and down. "Your lady friends aren't packing, so they're not going to stop me." He grinned and lifted a hand. For a split second Mason thought he was going to strike Hanh, but instead he put his palm over his eyes.

"Now!" Hanh shouted.

Mason saw Matt's eyes glaze over, and quickly

tried to focus on Hanh, imagining streaming energy flowing up through his core, out toward her. She lunged toward Ali, her arms moving up in a single fluid motion, and shoved his chest with both hands. She put all her weight into it, and he lost his balance and fell backward, into nothingness, a blur of lime-green winking out of existence. Even though Mason was concentrating on Hanh—she was the only thing in his tightly focused visual field—on the periphery he saw Ali disappear. Mason blinked and shook his head to clear his vision, to bring his mind back to ordinary consciousness.

Matt looked shocked. "Did we just ..."

"Yes," Hanh said. "You guys did great. It worked perfectly."

"Where did he go?" Mason asked.

"He's right there," she said, pointing to the spot on the concrete where he would have fallen. "But in the middle of the fifteenth century."

"Ouch," Matt said.

"Let's use the standing wave to get home before the energy dissipates," she said. "Back by the car, so we don't land in the middle of that construction site."

"Standing wave?" Mason asked, his head feeling hazy.

"From all the power we just used. Come on," she said, running back toward the parking lot. They followed her, breaking into a jog to catch up. There really was energy in the air, he realized, an intensity that he could feel prickling on his skin.

She stopped in front of her car and waggled her fingers impatiently for them to take her hands. The moment they connected, before Mason even closed his eyes, the sky went orange for a fraction of a second, then darkness fell and they were in the empty parking lot again, the three of them standing alone between Hanh's car and the construction fence.

Still panting, Hanh sat on the hood and pushed her hair back, grinning at them. Dazed, Mason looked around at the dimly lit parking wasteland, reassuring himself that he was in the right place. Everything had gone so fast. Taking a few deep breaths to calm down, he looked up to watch an airplane pass low overhead, landing gear down and wingtips flashing, seconds from touching down at LAX. His phone buzzed in his pocket, and he pulled it out absentmindedly. No one had called, but a notification read "System time adjusted to network time."

"It's two in the morning," he said. "When I did this out in the desert, I didn't lose any time at all."

"We drove in here just before midnight," Hanh said. "If you spend two hours doing something, doesn't it seem fair that it's two hours later when you get back?"

"I don't think we were there for two hours," he said, slipping the phone back into his pocket.

"Close enough."

Mason sighed. He found that exasperating, but he let it go.

"What'll happen to Ali?" Matt asked. He sat on

the hood beside Hanh, looking tired.

"He'll slow down, I suspect," she said. "There's no betting then, no racetrack—nothing to cheat on."

"He won't try to come back?" Mason asked.

"He's a nickel-and-dimer. He can't."

"What's a nickel-and-dimer?"

"It means he can't move very far—a day or two at a time. He won't be back."

"Will you rescue him at some point?" Matt asked.

"I guess I could." She looked at him thoughtfully. "But did he seem like a reasonable person to you? What's to stop him from doing it all again, or worse?"

Matt shrugged. "At least the indigenous people of this area were friendly. The Spanish said they were some of the most hospitable communities they ever encountered. He might survive."

"Isn't it a bit harsh, though, sending him there?" Mason asked, folding his arms.

Hanh locked eyes with him. "He was intentionally causing damage. That could not go unaddressed," she said sharply.

"Like she said, he didn't seem like the reasoning type," Matt added.

"You have to be bold, Mason," she said. "Not fearful."

"I'm not trying to be critical. I guess … it just happened so fast."

"I had to act quickly. He was trying to do a runner—you saw him cover his eyes, getting his mind focused so that he could time-shift. There was no other option. If I'd waited to talk it through, he would have slipped away, and we'd have to go after him."

Mason nodded and looked away.

"It's like the case you're working on," she continued. "You found that woman, so you have to be bold and take action—go talk to her."

Mason frowned. "Vanessa? How do you know about that?"

"It's a time sequence thing," she said, gesturing vaguely. "I can't tell you now, but I'll hear about it later."

He studied her for a second. "I didn't actually find her—I found her family's house."

"Sure," she said impatiently. "All I'm saying is, act." She glared at him and raised her eyebrows. "Seize the day."

"What else can you tell me about Vanessa?" he asked.

"Nothing," she said firmly, and stood up. "We should go."

Matt insisted on climbing into the backseat for the return trip. For Mason, the view from the front was worse, as Hanh drove even faster on the freeway than she had on the way out, if that was possible. They mostly rode in silence, drained by the experience. Hanh pulled up in the alley behind Pretty Nail Blowout and they climbed out, Mason relieved to be free of that car.

"Before you go, I have something for you," Hanh

said. "Give me one second." She heaved open the door and went into the salon, reappearing a moment later with two clear little bags. She handed one to each of them, and Mason held it up to the light above the door. Inside was a pill the color of day-old lawn trimmings.

"What's it for?" Mason asked.

"You're going to feel sick, from the time shift," she said.

"Oh, yeah. I remember—migraine city," Matt said.

"Is it some herbal thing?" Mason asked.

"No—it's morphine."

He stared at her, shocked.

"You have a legitimate health issue," she said. "It's not going to turn you into a junkie. You'll sleep better, and it'll take the edge off the headache. Don't take it until you get home."

He slid it into his pocket and said good night to them both, then walked around to the boulevard to find his bike. He wasn't feeling as tired as the two of them had looked, and rather than waiting for the infrequent all-night bus, he rode on the sidewalk and side streets, slowly making his way home.

EIGHT

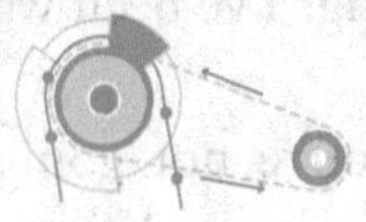

As quietly as he could, he slipped in the front door and eased it closed behind him. Not turning on the lights, he went into the kitchen, navigating the dark room by the ambient light of the city from the windows. He poked around in the refrigerator and found a pilaf Ned had made, then grabbed a fork and walked over to the French doors, standing there in the dark looking out at the city, eating the rice out of the container.

He was almost sated when the room lights clicked on behind him. He turned and saw Peggy, a look of alarm on her face. She wasn't dressed for bed, instead wearing jeans and a T-shirt.

"What are you doing up?" he asked. "It's the

middle of the night."

"What are *you* doing, lurking out here in the dark? You scared the hell out of me."

"I just got in. I was out with your boyfriend on a job."

"He's not my boyfriend," she said, scowling. "Not until I say so."

"Got it," he said, and then remembered. "You're going to the studio."

"Once my heart starts beating again, that's the plan."

"Can I tag along? I've been wanting to come and watch."

"Of course. You're not going to get any sleep, though, if you haven't yet. Are you sure you're up for that?"

"I'll sleep later. I've been told I should seize the day."

He took a minute to splash some water on his face and swallow a double dose of ibuprofen. The predicted migraine was starting to take hold, but he wasn't about to ingest Hanh's narcotic, which seemed like an extreme solution. He thought about flushing it, feeling the pill between his fingers through the plastic, but dropped the little bag in his desk drawer instead.

Peggy handed Mason a garment bag and maneuvered her guitar case out the front door, loading it into the backseat of her Prius.

"Is this your work drag?" he asked, hanging the

bag in the back and climbing in the passenger seat.

"It saves a trip home," she said, heading down the hill to the boulevard. "So what were you doing with Matt in the middle of the night?"

"We went on an errand with Hanh," he said, and explained what they'd done.

"Mason, that's crazy," she said. "Why is she the enforcer of the psychic rules? And who made the rules in the first place?"

"I don't know. Not every psychic can do the time-slip thing, and I suspect she's policing it because she's way better at it than other people. Matt thinks it might be a more formalized role. That's just speculation."

"So why can't this racetrack guy just do whatever he wants?"

"Because messing with causality can be destructive."

She didn't reply for a minute, focusing on navigating the quiet streets. Finally she glanced over at him, concern in her eyes. "It's not what you set out to do when you got into this work. Do you really want to be a cop?"

"That's Hanh's role, not mine."

She sighed. "Ned says you're going to start lying to your shrink."

"Why is he gossiping about me behind my back?"

"It's not gossip. You would have told me that yourself."

He knew she was right, but still, it was irritating.

"I have to lie. She thinks I'm crazy, and she'll get me locked up."

"I don't think it works that way," she said. "How can she help you if she doesn't know the whole story?"

"Oh, Peggy," he said, dismayed. "Please don't tell me you're judging me too. You're the only person I don't lie to these days."

"I'm just concerned—and don't you dare start lying to me. Have you considered looking for another shrink, if you don't trust this one?"

"Maybe," he said. "I have a lot of history with Miss Cassie."

The studio was in the old part of Hollywood, still rich with entertainment-industry production spaces that the big studios had long ago outgrown. Peggy pulled into a fenced parking lot beside the low-slung building.

"Andy's already here," she said. "That's his car."

Mason had helped Peggy connect with her brother, Andy, a few years back, and had spent time with him. When they went inside, Andy greeted him like an old friend. He looked a lot like her, the same brown hair, the same shape to their eyes, although Andy had a bit more weight on his frame.

"Are you growing out your beard?" Mason asked him.

"No," he said, touching his face self-consciously. "I just haven't needed to be anywhere looking civilized for a few days, so I let it go."

The recording space was behind a glass partition,

and Peggy stepped inside and unpacked her guitar as Andy sat down and got comfortable in front of the long console.

"Sit," Andy told him, gesturing to one of the other chairs.

"Where are the technicians?" Mason asked.

Andy smiled. "You're looking at him." He leaned back and swiveled his chair. "Technology has eliminated a lot of the labor. I can manage the recording and the mixing myself."

They watched Peggy getting set up, tuning her guitar and positioning herself on a stool.

"Are you a folk music fan?" Andy asked him.

"I like Peggy's stuff, but the genre seems a bit dated to me. I'm more interested in house music, dance music, that kind of thing."

"Mason, you weirdo—that's not music," Peggy said, her voice coming through the speakers in the control room, clear and crisp. Behind the glass, she had donned a pair of bulky headphones, and must have been able to hear them chatting.

"No computer, no music, toots," he said, eyeing her through the window and arching his eyebrows.

"Mason's music is so avant-garde," she said, "that he doesn't even go to nightclubs. He goes and hangs out in empty warehouses where the clubs *will* be someday."

Andy laughed, adjusting knobs and sliders on the board in front of him. They spent some time getting the volume levels right, and watching them chatting back and forth, Mason saw that they had built a comfortable collaborative style.

They started recording, Peggy strumming through the same tune again and again; in between takes, they talked about the nuances and the tweaks they wanted to make. Mason was trying to be present but struggled to stay awake, and his head throbbed. Eventually they recorded her voice without the guitar, running through the song several times. To Mason it sounded exactly the same every time.

The song was classic Peggy Pregnant, her wistful lyrics with a bright melody:

> I reached out, reached for your hand
> Looked for you through the years
> But we missed that connection, baby
> When you slowed down, and I shifted gears.

The fourth time through it, Mason closed his eyes, listening to her voice, the words forming images in his flagging consciousness. *Through the years.* The Barton Sugar Hill Trust. Vanessa's family still owned the house in New York....

"Are we losing you?" Andy asked, pulling his attention back.

Mason grinned. "Just lulled by the music. I love her singing voice."

"She's extremely talented," Andy said.

"She's also lucky to have you. I think her work is evolving with your help."

"Thanks, man," he said, nodding appreciatively. "It's good for me too." He glanced at Peggy through the glass. "Watching her play guitar is like watching my dad. There's no mistaking that she's my father's daughter."

Andy turned back to his controls, and Mason remembered the photos he'd seen of their father, the resemblance the three of them shared. He thought of the photo of Vanessa, her quirky asymmetrical look. She didn't look like anyone else. She'd never had children. Or had she? In a flash he put it together—either Meg Martel or Nissoué Louloune had to be Vanessa's daughter. It wasn't a psychic insight, just regular reasoning, connections in his brain sparked by Andy's words, but it was significant. He sat up in his chair.

"Andy, you're a freaking genius," he said, but Andy was immersed in the sound board again, tuned in only to the music. Mason spent a minute committing the idea to memory. Maybe that was it—maybe he'd found Vanessa's daughter.

It was close to eight in the morning when Peggy gently shook him awake. His head still ached, and it took him a minute to figure out where he was. She'd packed up her guitar and changed into her work clothes, a conservative jacket and trousers, her hair pinned up neatly.

"Time to go," she said gently.

"Did you finish the song?" he asked, sitting up.

"Part of it," Andy said, pulling his satchel onto his shoulder. "We still have to figure out the percussion, so it'll be another day or two."

"I can't believe you're going to go work a whole day right now," Mason said to Peggy.

"I won't be at my best, that's for sure. But it's worth it."

They walked out into the bright daylight. Andy gave him a bro hug good-bye, and Mason walked to the metro, which brought him a couple of stops closer to home, and then trudged up the hill.

Ned was sitting at the counter eating oatmeal when he came in. "That must have been some séance," he said.

Mason went over and embraced him, then sank onto another stool. "I should have texted you. I actually came home and met Peggy on her way out to the studio, so I went with her." He considered telling Ned about his insight, but thought better of it. Ned knew part of the story, but not about Mason working pro bono. He felt a pang of regret. That was the downside of keeping things from him—not sharing the difficult parts meant it was harder to talk about the successes. "It's cool to watch them, but they keep doing the same damn song over and over."

"I guess that's how they perfect it," Ned said, sliding the bowl of oatmeal toward Mason, who gratefully ate a few spoonfuls. "So what did Hanh have you do?"

"She wanted Matt and me to help her find a guy

in Inglewood," he said, omitting the loopier parts of the story.

"Did you find him?"

"We did," Mason said, trying to think quickly. "She wanted to have a word with him."

"Did he need a manicure?"

"Funny. He's kind of a misbehaving psychic. But she sorted it out with him, and he won't be causing any more trouble."

Ned frowned and eyed Mason. "You sound like a bunch of gangsters."

Mason laughed. "Nothing so dramatic. She asked us along for our psychic power, not our brawn."

He nodded, but in his eyes Mason saw doubt.

"Anyway, I've got a headache, and I haven't been to bed—I'm going to collapse."

He slept fitfully and got up around noon, still tired, but at least the migraine was fading. A pot of coffee and some fruit helped.

Joining Ned in the office, he sat at his computer and pulled up the map he'd made with the ley lines, zooming in on the line running under the Barton house in Sugar Hill. It was undeniably significant, to the point that just looking at it again made his pulse quicken. The next step was finding out whether Meg or Nissoué were Vanessa's daughters. Julia had insisted there were no offspring, but if Santos could produce photos of them, it might show the resemblance.

Alternatively, maybe the trustee could confirm it one way or the other. He checked the clock on his computer. He still had a couple of hours before the close of business in New York, so he put off phoning the law firm; he wanted to think it through a little more, get things straight in his head first.

Leafing through his notes and the printouts he'd made at the library, he stopped at the newspaper article that had mentioned Vanessa's roots. It was a puff piece, perhaps even written by a studio PR department, but it had some direct quotes from Vanessa. One line caught his eye. The author had asked her vaguely what her goals were, and she replied, "I want to drink deeply from the waters of life." It was a strange thing to say, but maybe there was some context that he was missing, some contemporary humorous reference now lost to time.

The turn of phrase reminded him of something else. He mulled it over for a minute, then pulled up the tarot book and searched it for "waters of life." It came up in the description of the Star card. In tarot, the waters of life symbolized uncovering truth or acquiring wisdom. He could easily imagine that, looking at the artwork on the card, depicting a woman pouring water. With a start he noticed that over her shoulder was a bird perched in a tree. It's exactly what he'd dreamed about—Anna, the great proponent of tarot, pointing out a bird in a tree, even calling it "the Star."

He got up and went into the bedroom, pulled

his notepad out of the drawer in the nightstand, and took it back to his desk, where he flipped through it, looking for his notes on that dream. It was exactly what he'd written: "The Star is in New York." It all fit together—Anna's pointing at the bird, the bird on the card, and even Vanessa's nickname—the Immortal Warbler. He chuckled, marveling at the overlapping pieces. Why hadn't he seen this before? The pattern seemed obvious now.

"What's funny?" Ned asked, looking up from his desk.

"I just figured out something for the case I'm working on," Mason said, grinning. "I love it when this happens."

He'd also made a note in his night journal to query Anna as to whether she had actually been there, in Central Park with him. The dream was significant enough that he knew he had to ask, regardless of how embarrassing it was. He did a quick Web search for Anna's shop, and soon found her number. He punched it into his phone and went out onto the balcony, relaxing in one of the chairs. Anna's familiar deep voice answered after a couple of rings.

"Psychic Center. How may I direct your call?" she asked, her accent stretching out the vowels.

"It's Mason," he said, stifling a laugh. He'd only seen Anna and her niece in the little shop, so he knew there weren't a lot of places to direct a caller. But it did sound professional. "I've been trying out the tarot thing, and I had a dream about you."

"OK," she said neutrally.

"Do you remember meeting me in the dream state recently? We were in New York, in Central Park, and you pointed out a bird in a tree."

"I see … I don't have a memory of that. Maybe we crossed paths subconsciously. Was the information useful?"

"It's significant for the case I'm working on. I wondered if you had any other insights."

"Not consciously. Some part of me might have been there, but it's also possible that your mind used me as a symbol of wisdom or insight."

"That makes sense," he said, although with her pragmatic business sense, she wasn't exactly cast in the mold of Minerva, or any other representation of esoteric wisdom.

"Too bad I can't invoice you for that," she said.

They chatted for a while about tarot technique and how he was using it, and she encouraged him to continue pursuing it. Finally he ended the call. He had to phone the trustee, even though he was brain-tired and wanted nothing more than to sit and enjoy the warmth and the blue sky. But he pushed through and looked up the law firm's number on his phone.

A receptionist answered, and when Mason recited the name of the trust, she transferred him to someone called Ms. Bailey.

"My name is Mason Braithwaite, and I wanted to talk to the trustee for the Barton Sugar Hill Trust," he told her. "Is that you?"

"The firm is the trustee. I'm the administrator. What can I do for you?"

"I'm looking into a woman named Vanessa Barton, who was a radio personality in the 1950s. I think the trust is connected to her."

"Who told you that?" she demanded.

He knew instantly that he was right—even though he'd never met her, and she was thousands of miles away, he'd touched a nerve, and he could feel it. If he'd been wrong, she wouldn't have reacted so strongly.

"My research," he said. "I know the trust is connected to Vanessa or her daughter." It was bluster, but he knew now that he was on to something.

"I can't discuss the trust or the beneficiaries," she said.

"I understand that. But some of it must be common knowledge. Is Meg Martel related to the Bartons? Surely that's not privileged information."

"Mr. Braithwaite," she said, sounding flustered, "I can't discuss any of that."

"Even the parts that are public record?"

"It's out of the question," she said, and ended the call.

He slid his phone into his pants pocket. She hadn't given him any answers, but she'd told him a lot—that the trust was definitely connected to Vanessa, or Meg, or her daughter, and that this lawyer might be personally invested. He'd thrown her off balance just by mentioning Vanessa's name. If it wasn't personal to her, she would simply have given him a perfunctory brush-off.

His phone dinged with an email, and he pulled it out again. It was from Danny Santos, with the subject line "passport photos." He eagerly scrolled down to the attached images. The first was labeled "Nissoué Louloune," a woman with sharp cheekbones, maybe in her thirties, with a slightly sour expression, but as Meg Martel's photo appeared, a smile spread across his face. There was no doubt in his mind now—Meg had to be Vanessa's daughter. Her hair was styled differently than Vanessa's had been in the black-and-white publicity photos, and she had only the faintest hint of a smile, posing for a passport photo, but the uneven, wide-set eyes were unmistakable. He zoomed in on them. It was uncanny—Meg was a dead ringer for Vanessa. Santos had included a dozen lines of text data about both passports, mostly computer gobbledygook, but it included the dates each had been issued, and Meg's was less than two years ago.

It meant that Meg might have been the one who posted intimate details of Vanessa's life in Julia's online forums, and probably meant that Vanessa really was dead. But it didn't explain why there had never been any mention of a daughter, and why her existence had been so well hidden.

The problem now was how to approach it. Julia would be thrilled to find out about Meg, but just telling her about it wasn't enough. He would have to dig deeper—Meg was living below the radar for a reason.

He looked up at the cloudless deep-blue sky. If only the townhouse was in LA—he'd just ride over, knock on the door, and ask Meg if she was willing to be interviewed for a biography about her mother. She might agree to that, or she might throw him out. Either way he'd have a definitive answer for Julia.

Maybe that was the way to handle it: go knock on the door. In a way it was crazy to fly across the country on an errand like that, but he wouldn't have to stay over; there were flights at all hours on the heavily traveled route.

He thought about it for a few minutes, looking at the sky and the city over the balcony railing, considering the idea. He thought about discussing it with Ned, but he'd almost certainly try to talk him out of it. Hanh had told him to be bold, to act, and it was easy to see such a trip as conforming to that laudable goal, rather than being impulsive or capricious. Overlooking concerns about the expense—so far he was working for nothing on this case anyway, and he was two hundred in the hole for the photos—the only major downside was spending six hours each way in a cramped airplane seat.

What had Hanh said, exactly? "You found her—go talk to her." At the time he'd thought she was generalizing about finding the townhouse, but now that he'd seen the photo he knew there was more to it. He looked at the photo on his phone again, looked into Meg's eyes.

He went back into the office and searched for

flights, and surprisingly they didn't seem insanely overpriced, perhaps because there was so much competition on that specific route, and the peak summer season was ending. He found a seat on a red-eye for tonight and a return for tomorrow evening, so he'd get there in the morning and have about twelve hours to sort things out. Before he clicked on "Purchase" he closed his eyes and waited for any warning or insight that might prevent him from doing it, but nothing came to his mind, so he bought the ticket. Now came the hard part.

"Sweetness," he said, turning to Ned. "How would you feel about taking me to LAX tonight?"

He looked up from his desk, eyes narrowing. "Why?"

"I'm going to New York."

"What? Why?"

"It's where this case is taking me."

"The dead radio star? Seriously? Where are you going to stay?"

"I'm not—I'll be back tomorrow night."

"Wow." He watched Mason for a few seconds, concern in his eyes. "Are you sure it isn't something you can figure out by phone, or at the library?"

"The library got me this far," he said, keeping his voice even. "I have to follow the clues, and they lead to Manhattan."

"I guess as long as your waitress is covering the fare," Ned said, folding his arms.

"Of course," he said. She wasn't, not yet, but it

wasn't beyond the realm of possibility, so it wasn't a complete lie.

Ned sighed. "I suppose you've already booked the flight, so there's no point trying to talk you out of it."

"I have."

He nodded. "I'll make you some sandwiches. There's nothing decent to eat on airplanes."

Mason spent a couple of hours on the balcony researching the trains he'd need to use to get to Meg's neighborhood, stations where he'd have to transfer, and where he could eat. Ned came out at one point and gave him a New York City transit card.

"From my last trip," he explained. "It should still have some money on it."

Ned made them dinner, a lentil curry with jasmine rice. Mason made sure his computer was fully charged before sliding it into his backpack, and then changed clothes.

"Is that what you're wearing?" Ned asked, looking him over.

"I checked the weather. It's still in the nineties there, and like, six hundred percent humidity. I'm not going to need a jacket."

"The tan chinos, though. If you have meetings, maybe you want to wear other pants? The East Coast is dressier than here."

"It's not a formal meeting, and I want to be comfortable. I was almost going to wear shorts."

"In that case, stick with the chinos."

Ned pulled the Barracuda out of the garage, and Mason climbed in the passenger side. A house music show they both liked, *Metro Grooves,* was on the radio, and Ned didn't say much as he confidently navigated the freeway traffic, the car's throaty engine purring contentedly at highway speed. Mason was glad that Ned hadn't opposed this excursion. It meant they could take this ride in amicable silence, and Mason felt free to go. He knew that Ned's twelve-stepping had taught him not to tell people what to do. More than that, there was tacit trust between them, despite Ned's skepticism.

Soon they were off the freeway and in the labyrinth of looping roadways at LAX.

"Call me when you get there," Ned said as he pulled up to the curb.

"No way. It'll be the middle of the night for you."

"Well, text me, then."

"I will." He leaned over and embraced Ned tightly, then climbed out. "See you tomorrow."

Before long he was lined up with everybody else, scanned and prodded, stooping to enter the plane, shuffling awkwardly in the confined space. He settled into his seat, next to the window where he could sleep without anyone climbing over him, his earbuds shoved tightly inside his ears. He hadn't yet caught up on sleep after his night out with Hanh, and he was unconscious almost as soon as they were in the air.

NINE

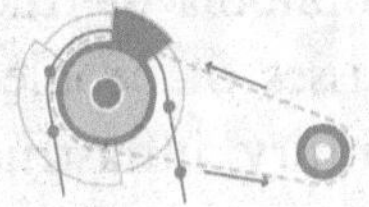

It took him a minute to realize where he was when his seatmate gently shook him awake.

"We're about to land," she said.

"Thanks," he mumbled, straightening up and wiping the drool off his cheek.

After he deplaned he found a coffee place in the terminal and bought two triple espressos, slamming one as soon as it came up and carrying the other with him as he looked for the rail platform. He swiped Ned's transit card at the kiosk and found that it still had more than twenty dollars on it.

"Thank you, Ned Vélez," he said, and found a seat on the train. By the time he'd finished his second coffee, he was starting to feel awake. When he went to the street level to change trains, the unconditioned air hit him like a wall. It was stiflingly hot for so early in the morning, and the humidity made him gasp. It smelled like Ned's sweet rice vinegar poured over the grease gun Steve had used to lubricate his device. Hopefully that was just the train station, not the city as a whole.

Once he was away from the airport it got a lot more crowded. The subway became more impossibly packed with bodies with each stop closer to the city center, and it was just as hot as it had been on the street. The claustrophobia of trudging up and into Midtown with masses of people was amplified by the nineteenth-century infrastructure—heavy iron beams, low ceilings, steep and narrow stairs. But there was energy here too, and he felt buoyed by the pace of the foot traffic, swept along with it. If Steve's thinking was right, the ley lines under this city must be especially energetic.

It took him a minute to get his bearings and locate a little vegan diner he'd read about. It was crowded but he squeezed into a table and ordered breakfast. He texted Ned while he waited: "Arrived in one piece. Having breakfast in Midtown," then read some news, sipping at a coffee. Back on the street he stopped at the corner to look at a map on his phone, trying to figure out where to catch the next train. He looked up when a man with wispy white hair spoke to him. He was waiting at a bus stop, and wearing a trench coat despite the heat.

"What are you looking for, Red?"

"The subway. I'm headed uptown, I think. Sugar Hill."

"That's *way* uptown. Take the A train—the stairs are right across the street."

He thanked the man and descended into the station, and soon was on his way north, riding the length of the little island underground. It took longer than he'd expected.

Coming up out of the station into the sunshine and heat in Harlem, he stopped for a minute on the sidewalk. It was the first time he'd felt apprehensive since setting off on this quixotic mission, and he knew it was probably irrational. But he rested with it a minute, and finally decided it wasn't a psychic insight, just ordinary fear. He pushed it aside and looked at the map on his phone, then walked up the boulevard, turning onto the side street leading to the Barton house. It looked like Sesame Street, except for the cars parked chockablock on both sides, constricting the street to a single travel lane. Bert and Ernie never had to contend with that.

Soon he was at the steps leading up to Meg's door. He considered taking a minute to detect the ley line, but decided against it. Its existence was secondary to finding Vanessa.

By the clock on his phone, it was almost ten. Personally he wouldn't open the door to anyone at that hour, but most people would be up and about, ready to engage with the world. He climbed up the steps and rang the bell, then waited in the uncomfortable heat, keenly aware of the patches of damp on his shirt. He probably should have formulated a plan in the event that no one was home. Why hadn't he thought of that sooner? He couldn't very well just sit on the steps and wait.

But someone was home—a woman pulled open the door.

"Can I help you?" she asked, and looked at him expectantly. She wore a white blouse and a print skirt, her hair in neat cornrows, and had the slightest lilt to her voice, maybe a French accent. He'd seen those cheekbones before.

"You're Nissoué," he said.

Her brow furrowed. "What do you know about Nissoué?" she demanded.

"I was hoping to talk to Meg Martel," he said.

"Never heard of her," she said, but in her eyes was the spark of recognition, and more significant, curiosity.

"You're lying," he said gently. "I just want a few minutes of her time. I've come a very long way."

He saw movement in the dark hallway behind her, and a woman's voice asked, "Who is it?"

"Some stumblebum asking for Meg," Nissoué said, looking over her shoulder.

She stepped forward, still behind Nissoué, but Mason could see her now. "You look just like her," he said. Her hair was neatly swept up, and she wore linen slacks and a summery blouse. She definitely had the air of money.

"I don't know what you're talking about," Meg said, but her eyes told a different story.

"I've been researching the Immortal Warbler of the Sierra Nevada," Mason said. "She must be your mother." He pulled his business card out of his pocket and passed it to Nissoué, who handed it back to Meg, not taking her eyes off Mason.

Meg didn't respond, but looked at his card, then back to him, calculating.

"Shall I get the broom to sweep out this trash?" Nissoué asked, folding her arms.

"That won't be necessary," Mason said. "I'll leave, if you insist." But neither of them were being dismissive, and their curiosity was almost palpable. "I'm here on behalf of a writer who's working on a biography of Vanessa Barton. I think she found something you posted to an online forum."

Meg looked surprised. "You'll have to go," she said, and Nissoué moved to close the door.

"I know where her Yappie award is," he said quickly. "I've held it in my hands."

"Wait," Meg said quietly to Nissoué. "Well? Where is it?" Her expression had changed—he'd caught her attention.

"It's awfully warm out here," Mason said. "I think I might be getting dehydrated. It's a redhead thing— we don't do very well in the sun."

"All right," Meg said, barely concealing a frown. "Come on in."

Nissoué glared at him with unmasked suspicion but stood aside to let him enter. Mason followed Meg into the front room, lit by tall windows that faced the street.

"Give me a minute," she said, and went into the back of the house with Nissoué not far behind her.

Mason stood near the fireplace and admired the room, decorated as a nineteenth-century parlor, with an eclectic mix of rococo and gothic furniture and ornate rugs.

Nissoué came back with a tall glass on a tray.

"Iced tea," she explained, her animosity now in check.

"I don't suppose you have coffee," he said as he took the glass.

She raised an eyebrow, but asked, "Cream and sugar?"

"Black," he said, and took a polite sip of the tea. Once she'd gone he guzzled the contents of the glass and set it on a coaster on the coffee table, then examined the collection of dour oil portraits crowding one wall. Most appeared to date back to the first Gilded Age, but a few looked even older. Several of the faces bore resemblance to Meg and Vanessa. A memory flitted through his mind, something Anna had told him. *Talk about her relatives, and she'll begin to trust you.*

"Ancestors?" he asked Meg when she came back.

"Some of them," she said, scanning the portraits.

"A painting really gives you a sense of who they

were. That guy," he said, pointing out a dark-haired man. "He looks so serene."

"He ought to be," she said, glancing at the portrait. "He was a wealthy man, and didn't have to work very hard for it."

"Still, it's only a superficial glimpse of his personality," Mason said, watching her. "Was he kind, or stern, or eccentric?"

"I know that my family tree was pretty eccentric— it produced both nuts and bad apples."

"Funny," he said. It was the kind of joke Vanessa told on her radio show.

She gestured to an armchair. "Have a seat."

He was glad she took the settee, a delicate-looking antique that might not have supported his twenty-first-century bulk. He pulled off his backpack and set it on the floor as he sat down.

She put his business card on the coffee table between them. "So, Mr. Braithwaite," she said. "Why exactly are you here?"

"Call me Mason. I was hoping you could talk to my client. Her name is Julia. I'm sure you could provide details about your mother that no one else could."

Her eyes narrowed. "That's all?"

"Julia has done a lot of research about Vanessa. She actually thinks she's still alive." He looked at Meg for a few seconds. "There was no mention of you, though, in anything that's been written about her."

Nissoué set a cup of coffee on the little table

beside his chair, then stood back by the fireplace, absently smoothing the front of her skirt. Mason took a grateful sip.

"If my name didn't come up," Meg said, "how did you find me?"

"Well, I did some legwork," he said, "but essentially it came down to psychic power."

Nissoué scoffed. Mason looked over at her, frowning. "You're a skeptic?"

"Not at all. I know plenty of psychics, but they don't look like you."

"I didn't realize I was supposed to be working a look."

"It wouldn't matter what you wore," she said. "You'd still look like some rando from the subway."

He glared at her. "What is your problem with me? I'm a full-on psychic *brujo*. Not a rando."

"That's it," Nissoué said, throwing up her hands. "I'm calling the police."

"Knock it off, both of you," Meg said, raising her voice. And to Nissoué, "I'll call if I need you."

Wordlessly Nissoué acquiesced and left the room. Mason could feel the color in his face, and willed himself to calm down.

"She's very protective of me," Meg said apologetically. "She grew up in Haiti, where there's a lot of corruption, so she's not very trusting. I suspect psychics look different there."

"I can imagine," he said. "I'm sorry for losing my temper. Is she your girlfriend?"

Meg smiled. "My companion. What do they call it now? My personal assistant. No romantic entanglement."

"Got it," he said, and resisted the urge to pull out his yellow pad to make notes.

"So you're a *brujo*?" she asked, furrowing her brow.

"That's just bluster. I wanted to say that I know what I'm doing."

She nodded. "I've run across lots of psychics, lo these many years."

Mason smiled at the phrase. It sounded odd, considering she couldn't be older than her mid-forties. Could that be right? he wondered. How old would her mother have been?

"Some are charlatans, some are legit," she continued. "You don't seem like a charlatan."

"Thank you," he said, and reached for his coffee cup.

"Your phone number," she said, glancing at his card on the table, "implies that you're from Los Angeles." She pronounced it "loss-*ang*-less," dropping an entire syllable, something Mason had only ever heard in old movies. "And you came all the way here to knock on my door."

"It seemed like the only way to get to the truth. I suppose I could have written a letter or something, but someone reminded me recently that life is short."

Meg smiled sympathetically.

What Hanh had actually said was about being bold, and taking action, but it correlated with life being short. Thinking about that conversation, he had a sudden flash of insight. "My god," he said quietly, his eyes growing wide. "It's you."

"Excuse me?" she said uncomfortably.

"I don't know how it's possible," Mason said slowly, "but you're Vanessa." A smile spread across his face. It made no sense that she looked so young, that she'd aged hardly at all since that long-ago publicity photo, but Hanh had said it: *You found her.* "You're the Immortal Warbler."

Fear flashed in her eyes. "Slow down. You don't know what you're talking about."

"Don't freak out," he said quickly, holding up his palms. "I deal with this kind of thing all the time. It's OK."

"Why are you really here?" she said, her tone agitated. "To toss outlandish aspersions around? I welcomed you into my home, and this is what you have to say to me?"

"I just now figured it out," he said, trying to sound calm and noting that she wasn't denying it. "I didn't come here to upset you. Julia suspected that Vanessa—that you—were still alive because of that forum post. That's what led me here."

She looked at him for a minute, and Mason held his breath, wondering if he was about to get eighty-sixed.

"Damn the Internet," she said finally, the anger gone from her voice.

"So it's true." He realized he was grinning like an

idiot, but it was hard to contain his excitement.

She sighed. "It would be silly to lie to you when you've ascertained the truth. You used your psychic abilities, I hope?"

He nodded assent.

"I am concerned, however. I've gone to great lengths to obscure any trace of Vanessa. The last thing I need is a parade of fans beating down my door."

"That's not going to happen. I can keep your secret. It's just so … unexpected."

"Secrets," she said, meeting his eye. "Sometimes they're hidden in plain sight because no one believes them."

"Absolutely," Mason said. "I know lots of things to be true that are widely discredited."

"Have you heard of morgeria?" she asked.

He shook his head.

"If you look it up, you'll see it defined as 'extreme longevity.' You'll also find that it's considered mythical, like bigfoot, or time travel."

"Time travel is totally real," Mason said.

She smiled. "So is morgeria."

"How old are you?" he asked, almost afraid of the answer.

"Isn't it interesting," she said, tenting her fingers, "that they called me the Immortal Warbler?"

He felt the hair prickle on the back of his neck.

She laughed. "To my knowledge, no one is immortal. But people with my condition regularly live for four hundred years."

He studied at her, doing the math in his head. "You look the same as in the publicity photos from the 1950s."

"Well," she said, touching her upswept hair self-consciously, "a wrinkle here and there; a few gray hairs. You can imagine the problem we have. We can't stay in the same place, have the same friends, while not growing older like everyone else. We have to move on."

"Is that why you walked out of the studio that day?"

"Actually, I was just sick of that job, sick of the producers." She looked away. "It was a mistake to let myself get that prominent, but those were heady times. The career made it harder to be inconspicuous. It's why Vanessa Barton became a recluse in the 1980s."

"And faked her death in 1998."

She frowned. "I prefer to think of it as switching identities. The woman born Meg Martel died at the tragically tender age of twenty-four. She was gracious enough to do so in circumstances that allowed me to assume her place."

"Did you help her with that?"

"Mason," she said, taken aback. "I'm not a murderess. Meg Martel overdosed in a shooting gallery a few miles from here, alone and estranged from her family. I had nothing to do with it, but one of my confreres happened to work in the morgue." She laughed and shook her head. "I don't know why I'm explaining myself to you. It doesn't matter if you believe me."

"Are there a lot of people with your condition?" he asked.

"It's very rare. But we get to know each other, and help each other stay undetected."

"Good idea," he said. "You'd be turned into lab rats."

"That's why it's optimal that morgeria is considered a myth. You could walk out of here and tell people there's a two-hundred-year-old woman inside, and no one would believe you."

"Is that how old you are?"

"I was born six years before the Revolutionary War, in the province of New Hampshire," she said, leaning back on the settee.

Mason considered that, and all the things she must have seen.

"What's your connection to the Barton family?" he asked. "This was their house in the nineteenth century."

"This has always been my house," she said. "I bought the land and hired the architect. The Barton money is money that I made, but of course until recently only men could own things. The original Vanessa Barton was a relative who died in this very house during the great influenza pandemic, allowing me to take the family name again for a time. I've always been the core of the Barton family, regardless of the name I was using."

"It is a lovely house," he said.

"Tell me about Julia."

"Well, this book about you—about the Immortal Warbler—is her passion, but she doesn't have the resources to work on it full-time. She's working two minimum-wage jobs and saving what she can to take time off later to write. She offered to pay me out of that fund, but I just couldn't do that. She's so sincere and so driven that I wanted to help anyway. I'm glad I did."

She raised her eyebrows. "So you're not even getting paid."

"Probably not." He smiled. "But I get the satisfaction of finding you. Would you be willing to let Julia interview you?"

"I'm not that person anymore," she said.

"But you know her better than anyone. Posterity deserves an accurate record." He thought for a moment. "I know you're interested in telling the Immortal Warbler's story, because you posted on that Web forum."

"I did, didn't I." She sighed. "Is she any good?"

"As a writer? She's quite talented, from what I read, and really good at research."

"How would I explain abandoning my identity? Faking my own death, as you put it."

"You don't have to—it's no one's business. Just talk about your radio career. Pose as Vanessa's unknown daughter, if you want."

"OK, Mason. I'll consider it," she said, and

glanced at the clock on the mantle.

"I'm glad. In the meantime, what should I tell Julia?"

"You're going to let me decide that?"

"Of course. I'm not going to blow up your life, no matter how good the story is."

"Thank you for that," she said. "What about Julia? If I spoke to her, do you think she'd be able to resist exposing me?"

"Julia already loves you. She'll do whatever you ask."

She looked pensive. Finally she said, "You can tell her Vanessa is alive, and I'm an old woman. Tell her you don't know why I faked my death, but that I'll call her, on the condition that she doesn't reveal that part of my story."

Mason broke into a broad grin. "You got it," he said emphatically. "She's going to write an amazing biography."

She stood, clearly ready for him to go. Mason followed suit, pulling on his backpack.

"The stories you must have," he said, looking at the portraits on the wall.

"Oh, yes. I knew people who were prominent when this country was new. Some of the people on the money in your wallet. Alexander Hamilton was a redhead like you."

"I didn't know that," he said.

"That was a long time ago," she said, looking up at the portraits. "There is a profound sadness in outliving everyone, burying everyone you love."

"I can only imagine," Mason said. He turned and walked toward the front hall.

"Wait," she said. "I almost forgot—where is my Yappie?"

He turned back. "It's in a forgotten room in the basement of the bank where Julia works. The building used to be your studio. Technically I suppose the bank owns it now, but if you want it back I know she'd get it for you. It's not like the bankers know or care that it's there."

"She sounds fascinating."

"You'll love her, Vanessa."

When he stepped into the hall, Nissoué appeared from the back of the house, looking somewhat subdued. As Mason bade them good-bye, Vanessa grinned and gently squeezed his arm, and he trotted down the steps, making his way back toward the avenue, unable to stop smiling.

On the way to the subway he found a coffee place and sat down with an espresso, collecting his thoughts. Tempering the euphoria of finding Vanessa was the realization that he'd missed a whole series of indicators that she was alive. Hanh had even said "You found her." It was foolish that he'd missed it. He needed to work on parsing the information, connecting the dots.

Pulling up his travel itinerary on his phone, he spent a few minutes looking for an earlier flight, and after a little work he was able to get it rebooked. He texted the details to Ned. That still left an hour or so before he had to head to the airport, so he took the train back to Midtown and spent the time walking around, admiring the architecture. There was so much more city here, compared to what he was used to, and far more people around. Eventually he found himself in Grand Central, awed by the vastness of the main hall. His phone rang, and he pulled it out to see that it was Peggy.

"Ned said you're in New York," she said.

"Yeah, I'm right up in it," he said, craning to admire the constellations painted on the ceiling far overhead.

"You just whipped up this plan since the last time I saw you?"

"It was a bit impulsive," he said. "I'm glad I came, though—I found Julia's missing person."

"Julia, your broke client? How did she manage to fund this excursion?"

"It's a long story," he hedged. "I feel like an idiot, though—I missed all these clues that the woman was here."

"You just said you found her."

"Not until I was sitting right in front of her. I should have figured it out sooner."

"You did figure it out, though. Focus on that," she said.

"OK," he said, and chuckled.

"So is this the first time you've been there?"

"No, but it's been a while. It's such an intense

place, and the scale of everything is so grand. But the people are short."

She laughed. "All of them?"

"Pretty much. I'm standing in a crowded train station and I can see over everyone's head. It must be like when you put goldfish in a small bowl, they don't get any bigger."

"I'm not a biologist, but I don't think it works that way with humans," she said. "So you'll be home tonight? Make sure your flight isn't delayed—the electricity is out all over the Westside. I'm not sure if it affected LAX."

"I'll check, thanks. What's going on there?"

"I don't know, but things have been weird today— two separate earthquakes, a bunch of outages. The minute you leave town, man, it falls apart."

"I doubt it has anything to do with me," he said.

Before he wandered back out onto the street he checked on his flight, but it was still showing as on time. Walking through the marbled public library, he admired its elegant reading lamps and glammy chandeliers, then found the train to take him back to the airport. Once he was through security he walked from one end of the terminal to the other, looking for something to eat. Ned's sandwiches were still in his backpack, he remembered. They were getting old, but with no other decent options, they would do; he could eat them on the plane. He gave up the fruitless quest for sustenance and went to the gate.

He was worn out, from the excitement of meeting Vanessa and from not having slept enough, but the plane had Wi-Fi, so once they were in the air he unwrapped one of his sandwiches and started perusing the news. Ned knew his palate so well— sourdough bread and pesto, vegan deli slices, and something that was still vaguely crunchy, maybe romaine lettuce.

The earthquakes Peggy had told him about weren't big ones, and there hadn't been a lot of damage. A photo depicted a chagrined shopkeeper wielding a mop in a store aisle where a couple of wine bottles had tumbled off a shelf and shattered, splattering the linoleum with puddles of red—but no structures had been impacted, and there had been no injuries. Strangely, though, the earthquakes had happened just a few hours apart on unrelated faults, one in the mountains near Bakersfield and other off the coast south of the city.

The power outage was even bigger news. Four different transformers had blown on the Westside, and three more in the eastern part of the county, all within a few hours. Terrorism had been ruled out, and the only explanation offered was that an electrical ground fault had somehow propagated through the grid, whatever that meant. Traffic was chaotic in places, and some schools were closed. The news story included a map of areas affected by the outages. It was odd how they lined up west to east.

One story about the outages had photos of one of the transformer sites: black scorch marks curled around the big gray industrial boxes, transmission wires broken and coiled atop the trashed equipment, workers in hardhats surveying the damage. At the end of the article he found a more detailed map, and looking at the incidents plotted on the streets, he felt a knot forming in his stomach.

Setting down his half-eaten sandwich, he pulled up the ley line map he'd made. The failed equipment lined up perfectly along the east-west line—right on top of it. He pulled up detailed coordinates of the earthquakes, and compared the epicenters to his map. They had both struck precisely along the north-south ley line he'd found. And the timing of the power failures, the earthquakes—it had all happened within just a few hours. It couldn't be a coincidence. What had Steve done?

The evening he'd met Julia in the diner, Mason remembered, Steve had talked about ramping up the power of the device. Mason typed a curt email to Steve, not mentioning the outages or the earthquakes.

How are things going over there?

He hoped there might be another explanation, but it all lined up too neatly to be coincidental. He really needed to talk to Steve.

Despite his unease he was able to sleep most of the way across the country, and woke up finally with the sunset, not long before they landed. He had a few seconds of peace before the memory of the earthquakes and Steve's ley lines came flooding back, bringing the queasy feeling to his gut. He sat up quickly and checked his email, but Steve hadn't responded.

⚙

Ned had timed it well—Mason saw the Barracuda approaching soon after he made it out to the curb. He climbed into the passenger seat and threw his backpack in the backseat, giving Ned a grateful hug.

"Happy to be home?" Ned asked, easing back into the traffic.

"Hell, yeah. It's a great city, but it's so crowded, and everything's so … big."

Ned laughed. "They were trying to build the New Jerusalem. It was supposed to be the center of the world."

"It has that vibe," Mason said. "The center of the country, anyway."

"Did you find the radio star's daughter?"

"Even better. I found the Immortal Warbler herself. Julia was right—she's still alive." He added, "That's confidential, by the way."

"Don't worry," Ned said, meeting his eye. "I don't spend a lot of time gossiping about your work." He accelerated onto the freeway, and raised his voice to be heard over the throaty engine. "She must be an old woman by now."

"You wouldn't believe how old she is," Mason said, smiling to himself. "The best part is that she agreed to talk to Julia."

"So you did it," Ned said, grinning at him. "You solved the case. I'm glad the trip was worth it."

❖

At home he took a quick shower and got ready to collapse in bed, but called Steve first. It rang a few times but went to voice mail.

"Just checking in," he told the machine. "I hope things are OK. Give me a call."

Sleep came instantly, and he didn't even notice Ned climbing into bed later. In the dream state he found himself at the bottom of a pit, a round hole in the earth. The walls were too high, too steep to climb, and touching them caused the earth to crumble. Above, he could see the night sky, wispy clouds and a few dim stars visible at the top of the hole. He turned around, the disk of sky rotating as he did, so far away, unreachable. He thought about shouting for help, for someone to pull him out, but there was no point. He was stuck here.

TEN

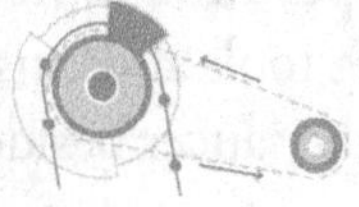

As soon as he woke up Mason checked his phone, but Steve hadn't called back. Ned had texted that he was headed to the Westside for meetings, so he had the house to himself. In the kitchen he got the espresso machine going and cut up some peaches, then sat on one of the barstools to eat at the counter. Once he'd woken up a little, he dialed Steve again, but hung up when he got his voice mail. He called Justine's office number. She picked up right away.

"Have you heard from Uncle Steve lately?" he asked her.

"Not for weeks," she said, "but that's not unusual. Are you two still working together?"

"No, but I can't seem to reach him."

"I wouldn't worry about it. He gets so involved in his projects, days go by before he checks his messages."

He chatted with her for a few minutes, but didn't mention the machine or his suspicions about it. After he hung up he drained his mug and considered his next move. Someone was humming, he realized—out on the balcony. Sure enough, Peggy was sitting there with her earbuds in, bare legs stretched out in the sun, reading a magazine. He made a second pot of coffee and refilled his mug, save an ounce that he poured into a proper little espresso cup. He found one of Ned's zesting tools and cut a strip of rind from a lemon, set it on the saucer beside the cup, and took it out to her.

"Yum," she said appreciatively, pulling out her earbuds and squeezing the lemon rind into the coffee.

"No work today?" he asked, dropping into a chair.

"The partners are having a retreat weekend at Ojai, so I'm taking a day too. How was your trip?"

He told her about meeting Vanessa and her surly assistant, not getting into the morgeria part of it. Even though Vanessa had said the condition was an open secret because no one believed it, he'd also promised to reveal only that she'd assumed a new identity.

"She must be in her nineties."

"At least," Mason said. "But she's in great shape for her age." He shifted in his chair. "So what have you got planned for the day?"

"Mental health care," she said, waving her glossy music magazine.

"Remember the guy with the rotating device in the backyard?" he asked, and explained his concern that Steve was connected to the earthquakes and transformer failures.

"Could his machine cause that kind of mayhem?" she asked, setting her magazine on the table.

"I don't know—but with every single one of these incidents strung along the ley lines, it doesn't seem like a coincidence."

She leaned back in her chair, tossing her long hair over her shoulder. "When we were out in the desert, you said there are no coincidences."

"I remember."

"There are hidden connections running through the world, you said." She closed one eye and squinted at him, holding her hand up, and traced a languorous spiral in the air with her finger. "They seem to swirl around you."

"I know." He nodded. "I haven't been able to reach him, so I want to go over there and make sure he's OK. Do you want to come with?"

"How could I refuse?" she said. "The whole story is so freaking nuts."

She got up and went inside to get dressed. A few minutes later Mason followed her out to the street, and they climbed into her Prius. Soon Peggy was merging onto the freeway, accelerating into the traffic.

They rode in silence, Mason feeling more nervous

the closer they got. Miss Cassie's words came back to him: *Are you making things better, or are you making things worse?* The shadow man had asked him the same thing. He hoped that hadn't been some kind of warning.

He directed Peggy to Steve's neighborhood, and soon they pulled up to his house, behind the Eighty-Eight. The place was dark, the curtains drawn. Mason opened the front gate and walked up to the front door, knocking and listening for movement within, then knocking louder.

Peggy hung back at the sidewalk. "Maybe he's not home?" she ventured hopefully.

"Let's go around back," he said, and Peggy followed him to the side street and then into the alley.

"Is that the device?" she asked when they came up to the back fence. Not much was visible under the canopy, just a corner of the supporting frame.

"That's it," he said. "I wish I could see into the garage. If his truck is in there, he's probably home." The garage windows faced the yard, not the alley, so there was no way to tell, and the gate in the fence was firmly padlocked.

"I'll have a look," Peggy said. "Give me a boost over the fence."

"We could go through the front," Mason said. "There's a walkway along the side of the house."

"Come on—we're right here," she said, and positioned her hands on the fence's top rail. It was only about four feet high, so she could easily hop over.

"I knew you came along for a reason," Mason said, looking around nervously to make sure they weren't being watched, then interlaced his fingers for her to step into and boosted her over. She landed on the patchy grass in an effortless crouch and walked over to the garage, cupping her hands on the glass and leaning in to look.

"The lights are off, but I can see a white half-ton," she called quietly to Mason.

"That's it. So both his vehicles are here." He looked around the yard. Sitting near the garage door was a plastic five-gallon bucket. "Is that empty?"

It was, and Peggy wordlessly brought it over and handed it across to him. He set it upside-down by the fence and used it to climb over, landing with an awkward thud.

Peggy had gone over to the device and stepped under the canopy. Mason followed.

The machine was motionless. The housing on top of the cone had been pulled off, exposing the motor and its wiring. The disk at the bottom looked different too: a series of oblong bars, each a few inches long with smooth rounded corners, all exactly the same size, had been attached to the rim. They were all metal, but there were several different types—some shinier than others, some dull gray, some darker. As he studied them he saw that they were all slightly curved, to conform precisely to the arcing edge of the disk.

"Isn't it supposed to be spinning?" Peggy asked.

"It was when I was here before."

She walked around it, examining it from all angles. "It looks so science-y. Like one of those Mars landers."

He pointed to the bars around the rim of the disk. "Those are the amplifiers that he added. They're made of different exotic metals."

She peered into the motor housing, then stood back and put her hands on her hips, taking it all in. "A scientific instrument that channels metaphysical energy."

"Ned would have a seizure," he said, and stepped back into the yard.

"Do you think Steve is inside?" she asked, looking at the house.

"It seems likely, unless he's down the block having lunch at the diner."

"Look," she said suddenly, pointing to the house.

"What?" The windows were dark, with no sign of movement.

"The back door is open, Mr. Psychic Detective," she said. It was, he saw. Just a crack, but it was open. "Should we check it out?"

"Yeah," he said, apprehensive. He went over to the door and pulled it open. "Steve?" he called, walking into the kitchen. Machine parts and tools were still scattered on the table.

"Bachelor pad," Peggy said quietly.

A glance into the living room revealed it to be empty. He thought about asking her to check the master bedroom, but that would be beyond cowardly. He steeled himself and walked down the hall, feeling his heart pound, and stepped into the room.

Heavy curtains blocked almost all the daylight. In the dimness he could just make out the shape of the bed. The lump under the disarrayed sheets was big enough to be a body. He wanted to leave, to run, but fought the urge and felt around for the light switch. Before he could find it, the bed creaked.

"Did you just break into my house?" Steve asked softly, his voice muffled by the sheets.

"The back door was open," Mason said, startled, but relieved that he was alive. "Are you OK?"

"Is that Mason?" he said.

"Can I turn on the light?"

"No. What are you doing here?"

"You weren't answering your phone, and I saw the news...."

"Did I hear Justine with you?"

"No—it's my friend." She had stepped into the doorway. "Steve, this is Peggy."

"Pleased to meet you, Peggy," he said politely from under the sheets.

"Likewise," she said cheerfully.

"So what's wrong, buddy?" Mason asked. "Are you sick?"

"No," Steve said, but he didn't elaborate.

Peggy finally spoke, breaking the uncomfortable silence. "Why did you turn off the device?"

"Mason knows why."

"It looks like you added the group-3 metals," Mason said.

"Oh, the hubris!" Steve said, his voice cracking. "I dreamed of sparking a golden age, and I wound up ripping the earth apart. I'm responsible for all those disasters."

"I wouldn't call them disasters," Mason said. "Nobody died, and the quakes didn't do any damage. Irvine probably needed a good shaking."

Steve snorted. "You know why they're so conservative down there," he said. "It was colonized by white Southerners after the Civil War. They didn't get to secede from the country, so they came out here and seceded from LA County."

"I didn't know that," Peggy said, "but it explains a lot."

"Do you want to get up and sit with us in the living room?" Mason asked.

"Not really," Steve said.

"Have you eaten lately?" Mason asked.

"No."

"Maybe you could get some takeout?" Mason asked Peggy, digging in his pants pocket for his wad of cash.

"Great idea," she said, and waved impatiently at the fistful of bills he offered. "I have money."

When she'd gone, Steve said, "I screwed up, Mason. I'm so ashamed. I overloaded the planet."

"Well, nobody got hurt, so maybe it's just a learning experience."

He heard Peggy in the kitchen, opening drawers and cupboards, then leaving through the front door.

His eyes had adjusted to the ambient light in the room, and he saw there was a kitchen chair at one side of the bed. He gingerly lifted the rumpled shirts and pants off it and dropped them on the pile of clothes in front of the closet, then sat down.

His mind flashed to the tarot. In this state Steve reminded him of the Five of Cups—so much gained but saddened by his losses. He made a mental note to read up on the card later. He sat quietly for a long time, watching the vague shape under the sheets rising and falling in the slow rhythm of Steve's breathing.

"Personally, I'm blown away that it worked so well," Mason said finally. "You were right about everything. You just underestimated how much energy the device would redirect."

"What if someone weaponizes it? I could see the military building a machine to harass their enemies with earthquakes."

"You're the only person who could have done this, man. I know what the device did, but no one else would believe it. It'll stay secret because it's so far-out. So unless you weaponize it yourself, it's not an issue."

"I'd never do that."

"Good."

Steve didn't respond, but he rolled over, still under the sheet.

"Did the device have any positive effect before you added the group-3 metals?"

"I think so," he said, his voice brightening a little.

"I think it was energizing the lines even then, I could feel it. But I wanted more."

"Maybe you can remove the new parts, and see how that goes."

"I'm not going to switch it on again. It has to be disassembled."

"Really?" Mason said. "It worked—too well, but it did work. It seems extreme to quit altogether."

He heard the front door open, and Peggy called out, "It's just me."

Mason got up and went into the kitchen. Two supermarket bags sat on the counter, and she was rinsing off a cutting board.

"I'm going to cook," she explained.

"You don't have to do that."

"I know. Sometimes you have to feed your soul rather than just fill your belly."

He went back and sat with Steve in the dark, asking him in more detail where he'd acquired the exotic metals, who he'd commissioned to cast them. Mostly he got one-syllable answers, but sometimes Steve spoke animatedly about what he'd done. The sound of decisive food chopping came from the kitchen, soon followed by the sizzle of a skillet.

"Whatever she's doing, it smells good," Steve said, finally pulling the sheet off his head. His hair was disheveled and several days' worth of beard had grown in.

"She's a very good cook," Mason said.

A few minutes later Peggy came into the room.

"There's food," she said brightly.

"Can you bring it in here?" Steve asked.

"Here's the deal," she said. "You have to get out of bed and sit at the table. I promise you won't regret it."

He sighed. "Give me a minute. I'll get dressed."

Mason followed Peggy into the kitchen, pulling the bedroom door closed behind him. Peggy had cleared the kitchen table of the tools and wire and esoteric metal parts and laid out three sets of forks and knives, even paper napkins. Steve came out a few minutes later, wearing a T-shirt and gym shorts, squinting at the daylight streaming in the kitchen window.

"Where's my stuff?" he asked, looking at the table.

"It's all in that shopping bag," she said, nodding to the counter. "Sit down."

"It smells like real food," he said, smiling wanly and taking a chair.

"It's onions and peppers and mushrooms," she said, "over veggie dogs on whole wheat."

"My god," Steve said as she set a plate in front of him. She put out similar plates for Mason and herself, and Mason dug in with gusto.

"You're a genius," Steve said finally, leaning back and wiping his mouth with his napkin. He seemed more alert now, more like the man Mason knew.

Peggy smiled, acknowledging the compliment. "My boyfriend took me to a hootenanny right here in town this week. It's all about roots music."

"Los Angeles has no roots," Steve said flatly.

"Well, one of the songs I learned is French." She stood up and pushed in her chair, standing behind it, and began to hum a melody and sway from side to side.

Mason chuckled, and Steve folded his arms but watched her with interest.

"You have to put your hand on your waist like this," she said, twisting her hip toward the table to show how it was positioned. "Not on the hip, but up at the waist. The thumb points forward, not back, which gives the neck a graceful curve."

"It also makes your butt stick out," Mason said.

"Exactly." She swayed and turned with her hand in that position. The effect was remarkably elegant. "The song is about unrequited love, so it's dripping with sadness." She hummed the melody and then sang:

> Mon amant me délaisse
> O gué, vive la rose
> Je ne sais pas pourquoi
> Vive la rose et le lilas

"It does sound sad," Mason agreed, even though he didn't understand the words.

"You don't know the half of it," Peggy said, and sang another verse, this time drawing out the syllables to exaggerate the sorrow, contorting her face as if deeply aggrieved. She dipped her head to one side, then to the other, dramatically flicking away imaginary tears.

By the time she was done, Steve had a grin on his

face. "Remind me never to go to a hootenanny," he said. "I'd have to start taking antidepressants."

"Roots music has the best kind of sadness," she said. "You get to share it with other people."

❖❖❖

A while later they left, and Steve seemed to have perked up somewhat, even pulling open the curtains in the front room to let the daylight in.

"Don't go back to bed," Mason said as they left.

They climbed into the Prius, and Peggy found her way back to the freeway ramp.

"Thanks for cooking," Mason said. "And for the music. That was amazing."

"There's nothing like a folk song to put things in perspective," she said. "You know, I think he might be bipolar. When you described him before, he was working like a madman, right? That would have been the manic phase."

"That does ring true. I don't think I could tell him that, though."

"Maybe you can mention it to Justine? If the family knows about it, maybe they can help him."

"Good idea," he said.

"Does she know about the device?"

"I doubt it, and I'm not going to tell her about it. There's no connection between that project and being bipolar, or depressed, or whatever's going on."

They rode quietly for a while, caught in stop-and-go rush-hour traffic.

"I'm glad he was aware that he'd overdone it with the device," Mason said. "Until the moment he admitted it, I wasn't convinced it was the device that had caused all that mayhem. It doesn't seem like a machine should be capable of paranormal activity."

"What about Hanh's car? You said it followed you on your time-slip adventure."

"It did," he agreed. It was a good point. And Hanh had said it was more than just a car.

"I've seen you do psychometry on keys and jewelry to get latent information too. Those aren't machines, but they're completely tangible."

"Sure," he said, and nodded. He was going to have to think it through. Maybe he had a bias against technology.

They were both tired when they got home. Peggy retreated to her room, and Mason went out on the balcony with his phone. He sat down and dialed Julia's number.

"I'm at work—I can't talk," she said. "But when I saw it was you I had to pick up."

"I have some news," Mason said. "Can we meet?"

"Of course. Can you swing by the bank tomorrow? I work till three."

He agreed, and she ended the call. He marveled for a moment at what great news he had for her: she was going to be able to talk to the Immortal Warbler, the object of her passion.

Back inside, he took his computer to the sofa and got comfortable. The tarot book had more detail about the Five of Cups. The artwork was dark, a cloaked figure with head bowed—reminiscent of Steve under his sheets—standing in a stark landscape. It was symbolic of useless projects and wasted time, according to the text, which is one way the saga of the device could be interpreted. He set the book aside and thought about what Peggy had said in the car, that maybe Steve was bipolar. It was a more lucid explanation of Steve's high at finding the node and building the machine, then the devastating low at the destruction it caused.

A while later he heard the garage door open and close again; Ned was home.

"Somebody stopped by the kitchen store," Mason said, rising from the sofa and noticing the heavy shopping bag in Ned's hand as he came in.

"It's a pasta maker," he said, pulling it out of the bag. It had shiny chrome plating and a hand crank. "What could be more fun than that?"

Mason eyed the device warily and kissed him hello. "I'll be happy to eat whatever you make with it." He sat at the counter while Ned figured out how to work his new toy.

"I hope you're not super hungry," he said. "This may take a while."

"We had a late lunch with Steve," Mason said, and told him about their excursion.

"I don't believe his machine did all that," he said, "but it's easy to believe he's bipolar."

"Peggy thought I should mention it to Justine. I

can't broach it with him, but his family can."

Ned mixed up a batch of pasta dough. Mason cut up carrots and broccoli for pasta primavera, and Peggy joined them at the dining table when it was finally all ready.

"Tasty," Peggy said, admiring a linguine noodle on her fork.

"Mason told me about your French song," Ned said. "Can you do it for me?"

"Of course," she said, and after they'd eaten she stood and performed the whole piece, hand on waist, expressing the tone of the music but not exaggerating the emotional content the way she had with Steve.

"Bravo," Ned said, clapping loudly.

She took a little bow. "Matt's hootenanny expanded my repertoire."

"I noticed that you called him your boyfriend today," Mason said.

"I guess I did. Just don't tell him that. I want to keep him on his toes."

Mason spent the evening at home with Ned, relieved to let go of his worry about Steve. He didn't like the idea of Steve trashing the machine after putting so much into it, but at least it wasn't going to cause any more trouble.

Drifting into sleep, he dreamed he was walking on a balance beam, like in gymnastics, but not nearly as high. His sock would slip on the polished wood, or he'd lose his balance, and then hop onto the floor. Peggy was there, and she walked the beam in her oddly specific hootenanny posture, one hand on her waist, the other raised as if holding an invisible torch, stopping now and then to regain her balance but not stepping off. Ned walked the beam too, confidently making it all the way and then shrugging as if to say, "Of course I can do it." Mason tried it again, and made it farther along before slipping off. Finally he took off his socks, and he did better barefoot.

ELEVEN

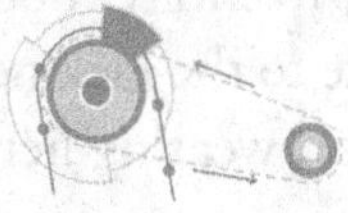

Once he was up and awake, he spent some time thinking about how he was going to present his findings to Julia. He took a yellow pad and a pen and sat out on the balcony. The biggest problem about not telling the whole truth was that it got confusing, trying to remember who knew what. A client who worked in HR had taught him the technique of going over a story in his head until it seemed as real as the truth, so it could be recalled as the truth whenever necessary. Perhaps she wasn't the best mentor, though, as she had absconded with a million dollars in public funds, and she and her boyfriend were still on the lam in Latin America.

Once he had the details about Vanessa straight

in his mind, he thought about getting paid. He had achieved what Julia had wanted him to do, but her circumstances hadn't changed. He added the cost of his flights and the cost of his time, then divided the total by the hourly minimum wage. Julia would have to work for weeks, maybe months, to pay him. He sighed and folded the page over. Peggy was right—if he wasn't going to bill her, he had to be content with that and not get resentful. He went back inside to get dressed.

It was the hottest part of the day, and he worked up a sweat cycling to Hollywood to meet Julia. He was locking his bike to the rack near the ATMs when she approached him, wearing her bank uniform and name tag.

"You look awfully pink," she said, grinning broadly.

"I'll take that as a compliment," he said. "Pink and pasty are my two skin tones. I tan about as well as a snowball."

She laughed and looped her arm through his. "Come on, there's a coffee joint down the block."

He couldn't help but smile at her exuberance. She must have known he had good news.

"Get us a table," she told him when they stepped into the coffeehouse. "What can I get for you?"

"A triple espresso."

"That's hard-core," she said.

There was an open table beside the window, and he sat down, pulling off his backpack and hanging it on the back of his chair, watching Julia chat with a little boy in line in front of her. He liked her, and he knew Vanessa would too.

She set his cup down in front of him and got comfortable in her chair, stirring sugar into her tea.

"So?" she said, eyeing him expectantly. "What's the news?"

Mason sipped at his espresso and launched into it. "I was able to find a woman in New York City that I thought initially was Vanessa's daughter."

"Really? How did you find her?" she asked. "Was it totally psychic?"

"No. I used your research as a starting point, then read up a bunch more in the library. I also have other sources that I can't reveal, people who do me favors by poking around where they're not supposed to."

"Got it," she said, and sipped at her tea.

"But it turned out not to be her daughter."

"Because she never had one. It was Vanessa," she said, her eyes growing wide.

He nodded. "You were right. She's still alive."

She threw her head back and roared. "Ya-a-as!" she cried, drawing curious looks from other patrons. After a moment dancing in her chair and chanting "I knew it," she asked, more calmly, "How did you know it was her?"

"I met with her. There's no mistaking that face. Plus she admitted it." He leaned forward and caught her eye, leaning in and lowering his voice. "Here's the thing. She's willing to let you interview her, but only on the condition that you don't tell anyone she's still alive."

She nodded vigorously, her expression serious. "Of course. I'm writing about the radio era—the rest is not really important. The world already thinks she's dead, so it'll be easy to stick to that."

"Good," he said, relieved.

"So why did she fake her death?"

"If you're not writing about that part of her life—and you can't—I wouldn't even go there. Focus on what you need to know for your book."

"That makes sense," she said, looking down at her teacup and dreamily swirling its contents.

An image flashed into Mason's mind: Vanessa and Julia sitting on Vanessa's settee, speaking intently, like old friends. He knew then that they would one day meet, and that Vanessa would take Julia into her confidence.

"So how will I interview her?" Julia asked.

"Well, she's in New York. She thought a phone call would be the best way to start."

"That's perfect," she said, leaning back. "It's more than I dared to hope for."

"I must admit, I didn't think I'd find anything, certainly not someone who was supposed to have died decades ago. I'm glad you convinced me to look."

She grinned happily. "So what do I owe you?"

"How about this," he said, wrapping both hands around his little cup. "I won't ask you for cash now, but I'll take a cut of your book sales. Ten percent of your net until I get twenty-five hundred bucks, and then we're even."

"That works for me," she said, grinning at him. "It means I won't have to deplete my writing fund, and I can get started sooner."

"It also means you have to write the book," he said.

"Oh, I will," she said confidently. "Should we write it up, like a contract?"

"Not necessary," he said. "I'll take your word." He knew she would complete it, and she'd do it well, because she was so passionate. It would be a great reference volume, but he couldn't imagine a big market for a biography of an obscure old-time radio star. Still, it felt good to support something that someone believed in so deeply.

She was beaming, and Mason thought of a tarot card, the Two of Coins, and its feeling of joy and industriousness, which, in this moment, fit Julia well. Anna was right—there was always symbolism floating around, always a way to connect it to the tarot. But there was much more to Julia than the ideas in a two-dimensional tarot card.

TWELVE

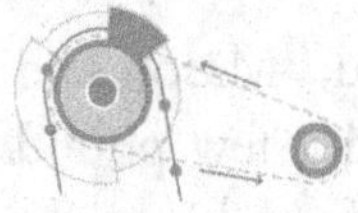

A couple of weeks later, on a sunny Thursday morning when the weather was just starting to cool off for fall, Mason's phone rang while he was having breakfast. He checked the screen and saw that it was Steve.

"Hey, man," he answered. "How are you doing?"

"Better. I never thanked your roommate for making lunch for me that day you came over, but maybe you could tell her that I appreciated it."

"I'll let her know. What have you done with the machine?"

"Do you want to come over and see?"

"Sure," Mason said, excited at the prospect. Perhaps he hadn't disassembled it after all.

An hour later he was cycling down the hill to the metro, and before long he wheeled his bike off the train in Steve's neighborhood. The familiar Eighty-Eight was parked out front, and the curtains were pulled back from the windows. He opened the gate and leaned his bike against the side of the house, and considered walking through to the backyard, but thought better of it and knocked on the front door.

Steve appeared momentarily and pulled it open, a broad smile on his face.

"Good to see you, man," he said, giving Mason a quick bro hug.

"You look good," Mason said.

He had gained a few pounds, and his hair had been cut recently. Even his beard stubble looked like it had been tended to. He waved Mason in and closed the door behind him.

"I stayed out of bed after you two left that day," he said, "and got on with things. I think I just needed to grieve for a little while after I overloaded the node. It didn't go the way I'd planned."

He turned and walked toward the kitchen. Mason followed, peering into the living room in amazement. The moving boxes were gone, and there were several pieces of functional furniture visible. The kitchen was clear of machine tools and electronic detritus as well, and though it still had the vibe of a single guy's place, it didn't look like a workshop anymore.

"It feels like you live here now," Mason said.

Steve laughed. "I couldn't do anything else when

I was building the machine. I've dialed it down a notch."

"Several notches, I'd say," Mason said, walking out the back door behind him.

The yard looked different too, with green shoots of grass sprouting in freshly tilled patches that had once been hard, barren earth.

"You watered the lawn," Mason said.

"I'm trying to act like I live here. It'll take a while to grow in."

The canopy and the machine were gone, and in the spot where he'd located the node was a round disk, a few feet across, painted dark green. They walked over to it, and Mason saw that it was made of rough-cut plywood, with brass lift handles from a hardware store hastily screwed into either side—no precision metallurgy here.

"You trashed the machine," Mason said, not masking his disappointment.

"Not completely." Steve stooped and pulled up the plywood disk, revealing a cinder block–lined vault. A much smaller version of the machine sat inside, spinning and giving off a faint hum. Unlike the original, it didn't have a cone, just the metal disk, smaller even than the wheels of his bicycle.

"You've downsized."

"Dramatically," Steve agreed. "This version should keep the node pinned in place without causing any physical damage. It's been running for a week now, and nothing has blown up in the vicinity."

"Will it energize the ley lines too?"

"It should, but the effect will be subtle. I'm not envisioning a grandiose golden age this time."

They watched it for a while, its calm rotation almost mesmerizing. Steve put the cover back in place and stood up.

"Did you ever install the backup generator?"

He shook his head. "I figure if the lights go out, maybe California can make do without my help for a little while."

Mason looked around at the new grass. "It seems like you've figured it out. Maybe you've started your own personal golden age."

When he got home, Ned called to him from the office.

"What kind of shenanigans have you been up to that would have drawn the attention of a Park Avenue lawyer?" he asked.

He stuck his head in and found Ned sitting at his desk. "What are you talking about?"

"There's a letter for you, addressed to 'Mr. Mason Braithwaite, Psychic Investigator,' from a law firm in New York." Ned nodded toward the envelope on Mason's desk and turned back to his computer screen.

"Maybe I'm getting sued," he said, picking it up to examine the return address.

"They would have sent a process server, not a letter," Ned said.

It was from "A. Bailey" at the law firm that

administered the Barton Sugar Hill Trust. He ripped open the envelope and found a check from the trust, for five grand, and a handwritten note:

Dear Mason,

I hope this covers the costs associated with Julia's research. I am thoroughly captivated by her. She's a firecracker! She reminds me of myself. Our interviews are progressing, and her book promises to be a thorough and skillful account. That pewter item we discussed has made its way to my mantel as well. Thank you for keeping the memory of the Immortal Warbler alive.

Meg

"Something good?" Ned asked him, not looking up from his work.

"Very good—money," Mason said. He sat at his desk and read the note again, smiling to himself. He'd have to tell Julia that she wouldn't need to pay him from her book proceeds, but he suspected she might already know about this.

The next morning he had an appointment with Miss Cassie. He dragged himself out of bed, pulling on his clothes and caffeinating, leaving the house when he was alert enough to safely navigate the streets. What kind of professional worked on Friday, practically the weekend, and why did it have to be so early in the day? Shoving aside his resentment, he came out of the metro and rode the elevator up to her office. The sign on her door read COME IN, so he slid it across to PLEASE KNOCK, pushed the door open, and greeted her, then sat on the sofa, depositing his backpack on the floor at his feet. She was at her desk but soon joined him, taking her usual chair.

"Do you remember me telling you about the guy who was into earth energy?" he asked her.

"Of course," she said, looking to her tablet and swiping through her notes.

"I saw him yesterday, and he's doing really well."

"I'm glad," she said, and frowned slightly. "Why are you telling me this?"

"You thought I was helping him act out his delusions."

"I never said that."

"Not in so many words. But he's not obsessing about the energy lines these days. He planted grass in his yard, unpacked his moving boxes, and got a haircut. I thought you should know."

"Is he still secretive about his hobby?"

"I'm sure he is, but that's completely reasonable, given the circumstances. He seems to have found some balance in his life."

She nodded thoughtfully, scribbling on her tablet.

Mason continued, "I went through this thing where I thought I was going to have to start lying to you, but I'm not going to do it."

"Good," she said, her eyebrows rising. "Lying wouldn't get us anywhere. Why were you going to lie to me?"

"Because I thought you'd have me locked up. A 5150 psych hold, whatever they call it."

"I don't have that power," she said, smiling gently.

"Even if you did, I want to move past the whole discussion about what's real. I'm getting better at my work, and it doesn't matter if you believe it or not. Maybe you say you think I'm deluded to keep me grounded—"

"I never said you were deluded."

"OK. The point is, I know what I'm doing, and I'm not going to stop doing it. I think I benefit from talking to you, so maybe we can set aside the issue of what's real and just talk."

She looked surprised, and set her tablet aside. "I'm down with that."

They did talk, and he left her office feeling better about therapy than he had in ages.

Saturday was a big day for Peggy. After all their hard work, she and Andy had finally finished recording her album. Andy was picking up the first copies from the press and bringing them over so they could all listen, and celebrate.

Peggy had picked up an old turntable at a thrift store and sat cross-legged on the floor, hooking it up to Ned's audio equipment. Ned sat on the sofa with his arm around Mason's shoulder, and Matt sat nearby in an armchair.

"I'm a little nervous that everything will still be

working once you're done," Ned said, but Mason could see that he wasn't, not really.

"Your amp has turntable connectors, so it's fine," she said. "What's the worst that could happen?"

"I suppose you could take down the power grid for the entire West Coast."

"Mason already did that," Matt said.

"Hey," Mason said, and laughed. "I was a mere accessory." And to Ned, "Would it bug you if we opened a bottle of wine?"

"Go for it," he said.

Mason went into the kitchen and found a bottle of red, pulling out the cork and pouring glasses for Peggy and Matt, and one for himself. He poured a fourth when he heard Andy knock on the door. Ned and Peggy mobbed him as he came in, grabbing copies of the album and examining them. Mason set the wine glasses down and took a copy from Andy.

"It looks good," Peggy said, flipping it over and checking the quality of the printing.

"It's beautiful," Ned said. "You did so much work."

Matt slid his copy of the record out of its sleeve and studied the myriad grooves. The cover image was a photo of Peggy that must have been taken at a performance. She was leaning in to the mike on a darkened stage, a serene expression on her spotlighted face, cradling her guitar in front of her massive faux belly.

"I can't believe I'm holding this in my hands," Peggy said. "My first record."

"You can be proud of it. I certainly am," Andy said.

"Let's listen," Matt said, and Peggy sat on the floor and dropped the record onto the turntable.

The sound was great, Peggy's strong voice and the wistful lyrics, and they drank wine and half listened, half chatted about the songs, and the production, and what came next.

"You seem relaxed," Andy said to Mason at one point. "Life must be treating you well."

"It is," he said. "I just wrapped up a case, and I got paid. I even got my shrink sorted out."

"That's huge," Andy said, and chuckled.

"It feels good to stop and take a breath, enjoy. It makes me think I'm getting better at this life."